Dear Reader,

Fairy tales have always had a special place in my heart—as a child, they were my first reading love and always the stories I wanted to reread the most. Of them all, *Cinderella* is my favorite. It has it all—an ordinary girl finding the man who makes her feel extraordinary, a gorgeous royal setting and, of course, the best makeover of all! To me, it captures the transformative power of love perfectly.

So when my editor approached me about contributing to a fairy-tale-themed month, *Cinderella* was a natural choice for inspiration. My heroine, Izzy, works around the clock as a cleaner to provide for her family, and when she meets a handsome desert prince, her life changes forever. I loved Izzy so much that I even decided to give her a twin sister so I could continue the fun with a linked book, *The Italian in Need of an Heir*, available next month!

I hope this book brings you as much joy as I got from writing it.

Love,

Lynne xxx

Once Upon a Temptation

Will they live passionately ever after?

Once upon a time, in a land far, far away, there was a billionaire—or eight! Each billionaire had riches beyond your wildest imagination. Still, they were each missing something: love. But the path to true love is never easy...even if you're one of the world's richest men!

Inspired by fairy tales like *Beauty and the Beast* and *Little Red Riding Hood*, the Once Upon a Temptation collection will take you on a passion-filled journey of ultimate escapism.

Fall in love with...

Cinderella's Royal Secret by Lynne Graham

Beauty and Her One-Night Baby by Dani Collins

Shy Queen in the Royal Spotlight
by Natalie Anderson

Claimed in the Italian's Castle by Caitlin Crews

Expecting His Billion-Dollar Scandal
by Cathy Williams

Taming the Big Bad Billionaire by Pippa Roscoe

The Flaw in His Marriage Plan by Tara Pammi

His Innocent's Passionate Awakening
by Melanie Milburne

Lynne Graham

CINDERELLA'S
ROYAL SECRET

HARLEQUIN
PRESENTS

HARLEQUIN®
PRESENTS®

Recycling programs for this product may not exist in your area.

ISBN-13: 978-1-335-14857-5

Cinderella's Royal Secret

Copyright © 2020 by Lynne Graham

All rights reserved. No part of this book may be used or reproduced in any manner whatsoever without written permission except in the case of brief quotations embodied in critical articles and reviews.

This is a work of fiction. Names, characters, places and incidents are either the product of the author's imagination or are used fictitiously. Any resemblance to actual persons, living or dead, businesses, companies, events or locales is entirely coincidental.

This edition published by arrangement with Harlequin Books S.A.

For questions and comments about the quality of this book, please contact us at CustomerService@Harlequin.com.

Harlequin Enterprises ULC
22 Adelaide St. West, 40th Floor
Toronto, Ontario M5H 4E3, Canada
www.Harlequin.com

Printed in U.S.A.

Lynne Graham was born in Northern Ireland and has been a keen romance reader since her teens. She is very happily married to an understanding husband who has learned to cook since she started to write! Her five children keep her on her toes. She has a very large dog who knocks everything over, a very small terrier who barks a lot and two cats. When time allows, Lynne is a keen gardener.

Books by Lynne Graham

Harlequin Presents

The Greek's Blackmailed Mistress
The Italian's Inherited Mistress
Indian Prince's Hidden Son

Conveniently Wed!

The Greek's Surprise Christmas Bride

One Night With Consequences

His Cinderella's One-Night Heir

Billionaires at the Altar

The Greek Claims His Shock Heir
The Italian Demands His Heirs
The Sheikh Crowns His Virgin

Visit the Author Profile page
at Harlequin.com for more titles.

CHAPTER ONE

CROWN PRINCE RAFIQ AL RAHMAN of Zenara strode into his uncle's private sitting room with an easy smile. Even bending his proud dark head in a respectful bow, he towered over the older man, who stood up in defiance of all protocol to greet his nephew.

'Rafiq,' the Regent said warmly.

'Sit down, sir, before you scandalise your guards,' Rafiq urged uncomfortably.

'You were my King at twelve years old and always will be,' Jalil informed him quietly. 'And in little more than eighteen months you will take your rightful place when I step down.'

The reminder was unnecessary for Rafiq who, at the age of twenty-eight, was chafing against the restrictions set down by the government's executive council when Prince Jalil had been invited to become Regent of the kingdom and raise his orphaned nephews to adulthood. Thirty had been set in stone as the date of Rafiq's maturity and ascension to the throne of his forefathers, but Rafiq had long been ready to embrace that challenge. Yet feeling that way troubled his conscience, because his uncle had been both an excellent ruler and a caring guardian—a man, indeed, infinitely more fit for the throne than Rafiq's late father Azhar had proved to be. Azhar's licentious ways and corrupt practices had plunged their hereditary monarchy into disrepute.

Without a doubt their parent's ugly history explained why Rafiq and his kid brother, Zayn, had had to endure a rigidly traditional, old-fashioned upbringing in which their every move had been hedged with prohibitions. Everybody had been terrified that Rafiq or Zayn might start revealing their father's traits although Rafiq himself had had little fear of that possibility, having been long convinced that his father had committed his worst excesses while in the grip of drug abuse.

'You said you had to see me immediately,' Rafiq reminded the older man gently, keen as he was to return to his own wing of the palace and enjoy a little relaxation before making an official report on Zenara's financial investments to the executive council. 'What has happened?'

Jalil breathed in deep and crossed the room to stand by the archway that led out onto a balcony from which a welcome waft of fresh air emanated and chased the heat of midday. 'I must ask you to speak to your brother about his marriage. He is proving…stubborn in the extreme.'

In receipt of that news, Rafiq stiffened and paled. 'You already know my opinion. Zayn is seventeen. He is too young.'

The Regent sighed heavily. 'I suppose that tells me very clearly how *you* feel about having been married off at sixteen.'

'No disrespect was intended,' Rafiq hastened to assert, discomfiture and guilt gripping him.

Yet how could he stand by and let his little brother pay the price of his own refusal to remarry? It was only two years since his wife, Fadith, had died but within weeks Rafiq had been approached by the council and asked to consider a second marriage. His marriage to Fadith, unhappily, had been childless and, although the medics had been unable to find anything wrong with either of them and had made much use of that catchall phrase 'unexplained infertility', Rafiq was still in no hurry to enter a second union and very probably go through the same torturous process again. He was in no mood to apologise either for want-

ing to continue enjoying the freedom that had long
been denied to him.

But, of course, that was not an excuse that his
uncle either wanted to hear or would even understand. Jalil had married young and remained very
happily married and, like the council, he feared
the sexual liberty that all were convinced had been
his late father Azhar's downfall and which had
caused so many scandals. Azhar had preyed on the
female staff and on the wives of his officials and
his friends. No attractive woman had been safe in
his vicinity. But Rafiq was neither a sex addict nor
a drug addict in constant search of another high.

'Zayn *must* marry,' Jalil responded gravely. 'He
must provide you with an heir.'

'In that case I will agree to remarry,' Rafiq
breathed in a driven undertone, grimly accepting
that he no longer had a choice.

He had withstood the arguments in favour of his
remarriage for as long as he could, staving off the
prospect of his brother being forced into a union
while he was still too young for that responsibility. While he accepted that his remarriage was
unlikely to lead to the much-desired heir, at least
it would buy his little brother freedom for longer.

'I will remarry,' he repeated. 'But only on the

understanding that my brother is given several more years before he is expected to take a wife.'

'Neither I nor the council would want you to feel forced into marriage against your own inclinations,' the older man protested in dismay.

'I will not feel forced,' Rafiq lied smoothly, determined to do the one thing he could to protect his kid brother from being compelled to grow up too soon. 'It is a necessity for me, after all, to have a wife. If there is to be a king, there must also be a queen.'

'If you are sure…' The Regent hesitated. 'The council will find this news of your change of heart very welcome indeed and who knows? In a second marriage a child may be conceived.'

'I think it is wisest to assume that there will *not* be a child,' Rafiq parried flatly. 'Of course, any potential bride will be aware of that likelihood from the outset.'

'Is there a woman for whom you have formed a preference?' his uncle prompted hopefully.

'Sadly not, but when I return from my next trip you may put suggestions to me,' Rafiq murmured, forcing a smile. 'I am a poor bargain for any woman.'

'A billionaire and future king feted on social media as the most handsome prince in the Middle

East?' the older man countered feelingly. 'Social media is *so* shamelessly disrespectful!'

'There's nothing we can do to silence such nonsense.' Rafiq shrugged. Both he and his brother had long been barred from such public forms of expression, closed off in every way from their peers. And the movie-star good looks that he had inherited from his very beautiful late mother, an Italian socialite, merely embarrassed him.

It was a tribute only to Rafiq's force of will that he had completed his degree in business and finance with an executive council who had refused to see the benefits of an educated ruler. In so far as it was possible within the restrictions foisted on him, Rafiq had had a normal education, but nothing else about his life had been remotely normal. He was always surrounded by bodyguards and he was sentenced to travel with a cook and even a food taster because his father had died from poison.

Rafiq was much inclined to believe that that misfortune had had nothing to do with sedition but was much more likely to have been the act of an embittered husband, a vengeful woman or the consequence of an unjust settling of one of the many tribal disputes for which his father had favoured his cronies or demanded bribes. Unsurprisingly, his late father had had many, many enemies. In spite of keen investigation, nobody had ever been found to answer for his father's murder. Many had suspected various scandalous causes to have prompted his father's death but there had been insufficient evidence to fuel a prosecution and, sadly, his father's passing had been more of a relief than a source of grief to the executive council.

In comparison to his father, however, Rafiq was not only honest and honourable but also a skilled diplomatist. Not that that had helped him much in his role as a husband, he conceded with a near shudder, so repulsed was he by the concept of remarriage. He had absolutely no desire for another wife. Naturally he didn't want to feel trapped again. He had hated being married and knew that his attitude was a visceral reaction to what he had endured. He didn't want to be worshipped like a golden idol either and he certainly didn't want to be cursed a second time with a woman who wanted a child much more than she had ever wanted him. Yet he had remained faithful during his marriage.

Only after his wife had died had he been able to discover that there were other kinds of sexual experiences, casual encounters that could be fun and occasionally even exciting, where both partners walked away afterwards without a backward glance. No ties, no regrets, not even an exchange of phone numbers. That was what he liked the most but so aware was he of his father's addiction to sex that he rigorously controlled his strong sexual drive and rarely allowed himself to indulge his physical needs. But when he remarried, he would *never* enjoy unvarnished sexual pleasure again, he reminded himself grimly, knowing that he was going to find a woman on his next trip to the UK and spend mindless hours in bed with her. One last sin, he told himself wryly as he took his leave of his clean-living uncle, one last sin before his life and his privacy were stolen from him again…

Izzy groaned out loud when she checked her watch. She was late, she was *so* late and if the cleaning agency she worked for learned that she had missed a regular booking, she would be sacked without question. And she couldn't afford to be sacked, not with thousands of pounds of student loan debt already stacked up behind her and certainly not with parents who were always in need of a financial helping hand.

In truth, her twin sister Maya did most of the helping out, but then Maya didn't need to get down on her hands and knees to scrub floors to make money. No, Maya was a real brainbox in the mathematics field, so bright she was off the scale and had started university at the age of sixteen. Maya had qualified for scholarships and grants and had won awards throughout her education and if she needed to make some extra cash on the side there was always some special project keen to hire Maya to juggle numbers and work her special magic. Unfortunately, Izzy had none of those advantages and had to do menial jobs so that she could chip in with much smaller amounts to help keep their family afloat.

Izzy didn't mind though because she adored her family, especially her little brother, Matt, who was disabled and in a wheelchair. Her father, Rory Campbell, was a jovial, optimistic Scotsman with a shock of red hair and a lifelong habit of focusing all his hopes on get-rich-quick schemes and then borrowing money when things went wrong, as they invariably did. Her mother, Lucia, was Italian and had grown up in a very wealthy family, who had disowned her after she fell in love with Rory, got pregnant and ran off with him, turning her back on a far more profitable and socially acceptable marriage to another rich Italian.

In truth, Izzy could not remember a time when money and debt had not been serious issues in her family. Had it not been for her parents' insistence that she and Maya further their education both girls would have gone straight out to find a job after finishing school. But in the light of that parental insistence, the twins had concentrated hard on getting good educations and focusing on goals that promised decent graduate jobs. After all, the main reason why their parents were so often in a financial bind was that neither one had had the benefit of the kind of education that equipped them for steady employment.

And while there was no doubt whatsoever that the twins' ambitious plans had been perfect for Maya, Izzy had found reaching her own goals much more of a struggle. Maya had gained entry to Oxford University, but Izzy was completing her studies at a local college in the same town, which enabled the sisters to share accommodation. She wasn't super clever like her twin and academic study didn't come naturally to her. Even worse, exams freaked her out and she didn't do her best work in that state. The need to sit the first of her final exams that very morning had been the reason she'd missed cleaning the penthouse apartment and in the aftermath of that daunting experience, she was wrung out and panicking that she had failed. Losing her job on top of that would be even worse.

When she walked into the elegant apartment

block, the security guard looked surprised to see her. 'What are you doing here at this time of day? It's almost lunch time,' he pointed out.

'I had an exam this morning. I'm running late.'

'I've just come on duty,' he replied, smiling at her because she was a very pretty girl, but particularly because she was also a very small girl and she was one of the very few women whom he could look down on. 'I'll have to check if the guests have arrived yet. I'm not supposed to give out the key for maintenance after eleven.'

'*Please* give me the key,' Izzy begged in desperation. 'If the guests arrive to an uncleaned apartment, I'm toast!'

'Just this once,' he conceded, stepping back to reach for the key and passing it across the desk, catching her hand in his to add, 'Fancy a drink some night?'

'Sorry, I'm seeing someone,' she lied, rather than turn him down cold when he was doing her a favour in turning a blind eye to her late arrival.

'Let me know when you're free again,' he urged with a wink as she stepped into the service lift that ran up to the rear entrance of the apartment.

In the lift, Izzy dug her pink uniform tabard out of her bag and donned it, smoothing a hand through her mane of tumbled red curls to prevent them from standing on end. She sighed, thinking she couldn't remember when she had last had a date. Keeping up with her studies, working several cleaning shifts a week and visiting her family at weekends left her with little free time. Indeed, a free night was a big enough treat and usually given over to curling up with a good book or watching a movie with Maya, with whom she shared a small dingy flat. Yet there was her father always telling her that the years of youth were the most fun-filled years of her life! So much for that, she thought wryly, wishing she had at least fancied the security guard because she had yet to meet any man who sparked her interest in that field.

Maya was the beauty in the family with her straight blonde hair, long legs and flawless face. Izzy was red-haired, five feet nothing in height and curvier than she liked. In the street men turned their heads to look at Maya and rarely even noticed Izzy by her side. The sisters might be twins but they were far from identical.

Inserting the pass key in the lock of the rear entrance, Izzy hurried into the apartment and extracted her cleaning box and the fresh linen from a storage cupboard. She spared the kitchen only a quick assessing glance. Although she would clean it before she left, the cooking facilities rarely required much attention because the tourists and business people who normally used the apartment either dined out or ordered in takeout food. As a rule, she spent most of her visit ensuring that the bathrooms were immaculate and, that objective in mind, she headed straight for the *en suite* bathroom off the main bedroom to start there.

Rafiq had suffered a very trying morning. An accident leaving the airport in the early hours of the morning had put two thirds of his protection team and his cook into hospital. Fortunately, none of his staff had been badly hurt but Rafiq had spent hours at the hospital and he was tired and hungry. He had been in no mood to deal with his uncle's panic at the mere idea that his nephew was abroad with only two men left to watch over him. The Regent had insisted that outside security be hired as a precaution even though Rafiq was only in Oxford to open the research facility he had funded at the university and would be flying home the following day.

A strange woman walking into the bathroom at the exact moment he stepped out of the shower was just about the last straw and he erupted into an angry tirade in his own language, demanding to know who she was, how she had gained entrance to the apartment and what she thought she was playing at.

And then he focused on her as he furiously secured the towel round his lean hips and fell abruptly silent, because she looked more like a child than a woman and her tiny body was rigid with fright and surprise, her face telegraphing her concern at the blunder she had made.

Izzy came to a dead halt as she registered too late that the bathroom was actually occupied and a huge bronzed guy in a very small white towel was stalking out of the shower to confront her for her impertinence. She stared at him in shock, her stomach turning over, and she couldn't stop staring because he was—*literally*—the most beautiful man she had ever seen. A shock of black tousled hair enhanced his extraordinary dark deep-set amber-gold eyes. He had lashes long enough for a woman to trip on, blade-sharp cheekbones that rivalled a supermodel's and a five o'clock shadow that huskily accentuated his strong masculine jaw line and wide sensual mouth. He was gorgeous. Even as that inappropriate thought occurred to her, hard hands were clamping into her shoulders from behind and pulling her backwards and her face was burning up with embarrassment.

'I'm so sorry!' she began apologising. 'I thought the apartment was empty.'

'Who are you?' Rafiq demanded impatiently.

'The cleaning and changeover service,' Izzy confided, shooting a glance to either side of her at the man mountains holding her fast. 'Steady on, guys. I'm not about to attack anyone!'

'How did you get in?' Rafiq shot at her while also directing the overzealous guards to loosen their grip on her. She reminded him of a doll with her white porcelain skin, bright blue eyes and that strangely coloured hair that brought to mind highly polished copper, a wild mop of curls spiralling around her heart-shaped face like question marks and tumbling to her shoulders. But she was not the child he had initially assumed, he registered, scanning the ripe full curve of her breasts and hips with a hunger that he struggled to master because it had been way too long since he had had company in his bed.

'W-with the pass key.'

An exchange in a foreign language took place over her head.

'You could not have come through the front door without being seen,' Rafiq countered.

'I'm not supposed to use the front door,' Izzy

argued. 'I used the service entrance off the kitchen—'

Another incomprehensible vocal exchange took place.

'We were not aware that the apartment had a second entrance,' Rafiq admitted gravely, shifting a large brown hand in an imperious gesture to indicate that she should be removed from his presence.

'Look, I'm *really* sorry about the mistake. I shouldn't have been here this late in the day but if you report me, I'll lose my job!' Izzy exclaimed.

'And why would I care about that?' Rafiq asked, stalking lazily into the bedroom as lithe as a panther prowling through the jungle.

'Because I've already had a really horrible day! I'm sitting my final exams and I ran out of time before I could finish the paper, so I might've failed,' Izzy told him flatly.

'You're a student?'

Izzy nodded jerkily.

'Wait next door while I get dressed,' he instructed. 'I'll speak to you then.'

Izzy drew in a quivering breath, deposited her pile of fresh linen on the ottoman at the end of the bed and backed out, the two goons on her heels.

'Can you cook?' the guy in the towel asked her abruptly.

Izzy blinked in bewilderment and turned her head. 'Yes…er…but why?'

'Later.' As she was herded into the spacious reception area, the bedroom door thudded shut behind her.

'You sit there,' one of the goons told her in a thick accent.

'I'll get on with my job,' Izzy overruled without hesitation, trundling her box of cleaning supplies into the other bathroom to start work.

Why on earth had he asked her if she could cook? Of course, she could cook. Learning had been a necessity with a mother who could barely handle toast without burning it. Both she and Maya had been making meals from an early age. Even her father was handier in the kitchen than her mother was, but she didn't blame her mother for that failing because in all the ways that mattered in making children feel loved, appreciated and safe, Lucia Campbell excelled, she thought fondly.

She would finish the bathroom, head into the kitchen and then hopefully the bedroom would be free for her to change the bed, she planned, refusing to allow her brain to dwell on what had occurred…that guy, that totally unbelievably, indescribably gorgeous guy. Izzy blinked, shocked and mortified by her brain's inability to suppress the images still shooting through it on constant re-peat. Yes, like any normal woman she noticed at-tractive men but certainly not to the extent she had noticed bathroom guy, whose wide-shouldered, lean-hipped, long-legged perfection had imprinted on her like ink she couldn't wash off.

In fact, until that very day she had never re-alised that a guy in all his half-naked splendour could even appeal to her in such a very physical way. She had truly believed that she was a little cool on that side of things because no previous man had ever sent an embarrassing flush of heat washing through her entire body and welded her attention to him as though there were nothing else but him. There in the midst of her most embar-rassing moment she had been wholly mesmerised by those eyes of his, those hard, dark perfect fea-tures, that sleek bronzed torso indented with lean muscles that shifted with his every movement, not to mention the fabled V that ran down from his hip bones… Sucking in a steadying breath, Izzy blanked her mind and got on with the cleaning while scolding herself for behaving like a convent schoolgirl who had never seen a real man before.

There she was, an unapologetic feminist being sexist in the most mortifying way, she thought, shamefaced. She had objectified 'bathroom guy' in exactly the same way women complained that men did women, without seeing him as a person, an individual. And sheer lust had dug painful claws into her body, her nipples snapping taut, an awareness she had never felt before slicking over every inch of her exposed skin as insidious heat curled up from her core. It had been mind-blowing, terrifying to feel gripped by something that seemed so much stronger than she was. She had never dreamt that sexual attraction could be that powerful or that instantaneous. Way out of control, not at all the sort of thing she had ever expected to feel.

She had always been far too sensible for stuff of that nature, not remotely like Maya, who, for all her genius, remained a romantic dreamer at heart. No, Izzy was a realist and knew very well that such a very good-looking man would never look back at her with the same hunger. She also suspected that he was, very probably, another woman's husband or boyfriend and guilt at that likelihood made her shudder at his effect on her. He was far too spectacular to be running around on his own, she thought crazily. No, had he belonged to Izzy he wouldn't have got more than twenty feet from her and he certainly wouldn't be stepping almost naked out of a shower in front of some random strange woman!

Rafiq strode out of the bedroom in search of his quarry and asked one of his guards where she was.

'She doesn't listen to orders,' he was told.

Rafiq grinned at the sight of her bending over the bath, her peachy bottom twitching as she energetically scrubbed it. He had never gone for really skinny women. He loved curves and softness and femininity. The lush feminine swell of flesh above and below her tiny waist turned him on hard and fast. He checked his watch and lounged in the doorway. 'So,' he murmured softly, making her jump nervously and twist round. 'Can you cook an omelette?'

Rattled at being taken by surprise yet again, Izzy threw back her stiff shoulders, wishing for only the fiftieth time in recent years that she were tall enough to be taken seriously and not so small that she was regularly taken for an adolescent rather than the woman of twenty-one years that she actually was.

'Yes…but why would you ask me that?' she asked impatiently as she swung round to be welded to the spot by dark-as-midnight velvet eyes that had remarkable intensity.

Her mouth ran dry. He was lodged in the doorway, rampantly masculine in his infuriatingly complete relaxation.

'I want you to cook for me. You have an hour before I have to go out to keep my appointment.'

'Why wouldn't you just order food in?' Izzy prompted in wonderment.

'I don't eat junk food. I like a freshly cooked meal served in private,' Rafiq told her, strangely entertained by the new experience of being treated like an equal by someone who clearly had not the smallest suspicion of his true status.

'I'm only here to clean and change beds,' Izzy pointed out abstractedly, taken aback by the demand.

'But I could throw you out of here and complain about your intrusion if I so desired and you could lose your job,' Rafiq reminded her with silken immediacy. 'In return for my generosity in overlooking that offence, you could cook lunch for me and everybody will be happy.'

'Is that so?' Izzy gasped, shattered by the ease with which that blatant blackmail attempt had emerged from his perfectly shaped lips.

'And if lunch is good, you can also cook dinner for me this evening and I will pay you handsomely for your services,' Rafiq completed levelly.

'How handsome is handsome?' Izzy pressed tautly.

Rafiq almost laughed at her upward glance of

sudden interest. 'I'm very generous when it's a question of my comfort and convenience away from home.'

Izzy nodded slowly. 'So, I'll cook lunch.'

'I thought you would argue.'

Izzy rolled her bright blue eyes. 'Not a chance if you're offering to pay me and keep quiet about my late arrival here. I'm not too proud to admit that I'm as poor as a church mouse and that when money talks, I listen.'

Rafiq liked her frankness even if he was a little turned off by it. Of course, he was accustomed to gold-diggers with a little more flair at hiding their true natures, the type that admired diamond jewellery, designer clothing or dropped loaded hints to ensure that they benefitted richly from any time they spent in his bed. Yet the minute his thoughts went in that judgmental direction, he was angry with himself. This particular woman was an ordinary woman working in an equally ordinary job to make a living, a person far removed from the polished models and spoiled socialites of his experience. On her terms, money was a basic need to cover real-world expenses like shelter and food and clothing.

'You said I've got an hour?' Izzy checked, peeling her tunic off up over her head, copper curls bouncing as she went for the challenge. 'There's no food here but there's a supermarket across the street. You'll have to tell me your likes and dislikes first.'

With difficulty, Rafiq dragged his attention from the bounce of her full breasts beneath her faded tee shirt as she removed the overall. His groin throbbed as though a blowtorch had been turned on him, the hunger, the need almost painful and at that moment he reached a decision. If everything went the way it should, he would take her to his bed and spend the night with her. Cruising clubs for a suitable pickup wasn't really his thing. Drunken or loud women turned him off. His guards drew attention to him. Photos would be taken. Discretion was always a problem. Conscious that those sapphire-bright eyes were still locked to him with an air of expectancy, Rafiq stopped plotting and replied.

Izzy checked her watch. 'First, shopping,' she told him.

'One of my guards will accompany you,' Rafiq informed her.

'That's really not necessary.'

The dark eyes went cool and hard. 'I decide what's necessary around here.'

'Oh…' Izzy succumbed to an involuntary grin

as if his innate dominance was somehow amusing. 'Do you want me to call you "sir"?'

Rafiq thought about it since, after all, that *was* what he was accustomed to in company. Yet, there was something ridiculously refreshing about her playful irreverence. It lightened his mood and stimulated his sense of humour because he had not the slightest doubt that she'd be 'sir'-ing him all the way if she knew that he was a crown prince.

'No. You may call me Rafiq,' he informed her smoothly.

'Do you live in the UK?'

'No. I live in Zenara,' he divulged with greater reluctance.

But Izzy wasn't even looking at him; she was gathering up her cleaning tools. 'Never heard of it,' she told him apologetically.

'It's in the Middle East,' Rafiq felt moved to explain with amusement. 'I gather you're not a geography student.'

'No, I'm doing English. My final year, final exams,' she burbled with a wince, sidling past him, her hip bumping his. 'Sorry, but I had better get on with that shopping…'

And just like that Rafiq's attention was dismissed by a woman. Irritation and surprise and something perilously like pleasure warred within him because a woman had never walked away from him before. No, they *always* lingered, chatting, flirting, batting eyelashes and desperately trying to hold his interest. She wouldn't be a pushover, that was for sure, he acknowledged with satisfaction, at that moment loving the prospect of a challenge.

As soon as she crossed the street, a hefty bodyguard at her side, Izzy unfurled her cheap mobile phone and rang her sister, Maya. *'Well,'* she said cheerfully in a voice laden with sisterly mystery and promise. 'Have I got a story to tell...'

CHAPTER TWO

'I'M NOT USED to you describing a guy as "hot",' Maya complained worriedly. 'Are you sure you'll be safe with him in that apartment? Is he the sleazy type? All over you like a rash?'

'Totally not. I'm not even sure he's noticed I'm female,' Izzy burbled, with the phone tucked between her chin and neck as she settled eggs and butter into the trolley, which was being steered by the guard. He had looked at her aghast when she'd thrust it at him. But as far as she was concerned if she was stuck with him, he might as well make himself useful. 'I was just there in the right place at the right moment when he wanted a cook, and you know we need the money.'

'Don't we always?' Maya sighed. 'Look, I'm heading home for a couple of nights. Mum has a chest infection and she'll need help with Matt for a couple of days. It's not serious but you know how out of breath and tired she gets.'

Izzy nodded while piling vegetables into the trolley for a side salad. 'Give them my love,' she urged, cruising by the milk and then the coffee, adding sugar and then condiments, reminding herself that she was returning to a totally empty kitchen while wondering if she should be shopping for dinner ingredients as well. No, for that she would require the official stamp of approval, she decided, because he might be a really picky eater, in fact probably was…for goodness' sake, who didn't eat takeout food? Nobody *she* had ever met.

On the other hand, she had never met anyone who used bodyguards either. What was the security all about? Maybe he was a diamond dealer? A dangerous criminal with a lot of enemies? An assassin on a top-secret government mission? Izzy entertained herself with such colourful ideas while she finished the shopping, anxiously checking her watch because the time limit Rafiq had given her was approaching fast.

It was a relief when the guard pulled out a card to pay at the checkout and, suddenly, she realised why he had been sent with her. Izzy flushed, embarrassed that she had contrived to overlook the reality that she wouldn't have been able to cover the costs that week because she had had to cut back on shifts while swotting for her finals. Once again

Maya was picking up the slack because her earning power was so much greater and Maya had already almost completed her doctorate. Still, Izzy only had one more year of living on a student budget to face, she reminded herself, but, of course, that plan was reliant on her passing her degree at an acceptable level...

There was no sign of Rafiq when she returned to the apartment and whirled around the kitchen like a maniac, quickly discovering the deficiencies of a kitchen space that nobody really expected to see much actual use. And when, rising above those deficiencies, she slid a bowl of side salad and a plate containing a perfect crisp golden omelette down on the table in front of him, she was justifiably proud of her achievement, but it still wasn't what she would have considered to be an appropriate meal for a powerfully built man who stood at well over six feet tall.

'You should've asked for something more filling,' she scolded him helplessly. 'I could have bought sourdough or added potatoes or rice. Of course, maybe you watch your weight or count carbs or something...'

As her flood of speculation dragged to a halt, their eyes collided and for Izzy it was like being speared by a trident. Suddenly her chest was con-

stricted, and she couldn't breathe and the saliva in
her mouth had dried up and her heart was hammering fit to burst.

'*Are* there men who count carbs?' Rafiq asked
with sudden interest, utterly ignoring the hovering guard who was supposed to first taste every
dish set in front of his Prince and hoping he took
the hint that that rule was finally being broken.

'The bodybuilding ones do. For goodness' sake,
I know men who wear more make-up than I do!'

Deeply entertained by the conversation, because
the people he met were usually very careful to
steer the dialogue through safe, very conservative
and often boring channels calculated not to offend
him in any way, Rafiq sent her a flashing smile
of appreciation. 'Sit down and talk to me while I
eat,' he urged.

Taken aback by the suggestion and spellbound
by that smile that lit up his lean, darkly handsome
face like the sun, Izzy hovered, feeling overheated
and oddly boneless as if her knees had somehow
lost all necessary contact with her lower legs and
feet. 'Well…er… I was about to make you coffee
and you haven't much time.'

'Skip the coffee. The water is fine and the omelette is superb,' Rafiq asserted, leaning back to
yank out the dining chair to his right. '*Sit,*' he said

again. 'Do you realise that I don't even know your name yet?'

'Izzy Campbell. Izzy is short for Isabel but I've been called Izzy since I was a baby.' Stiff with indecision, Izzy settled down into the seat. She was so close to him that she could smell him, and he emanated an inexplicably attractive aroma of sandalwood and soap and clean fresh male. For a split second she was tempted to bury her nose in him as if he were a pile of fresh laundry and colour ran up her throat to tinge her cheeks. He affected her in the weirdest ways, she acknowledged ruefully.

'So, tell me about the men who wear make-up,' Rafiq encouraged in the humming silence, recognising her discomfiture but spellbound by the strong zing of sexual attraction dancing in the air between them. On her part, it seemed so natural, so real, so utterly unforced and practised.

His lashes were as long and lush as black velvet fringes, Izzy noticed abstractedly as she told him about an acquaintance who, to impress a girl, had had a spray tan done in such a way as to fake the muscle definition he lacked, and Rafiq laughed in seeming astonishment. As well he might, Izzy conceded, when his own body was a masculine work of art, roped with lines of lean, strong muscle and hard abdominal definition. And then she

mentioned a good friend who regularly used eye-
liner to accentuate his pretty blue eyes.

With a sigh of annoyance, Rafiq checked the
time on his phone and thrust away his empty plate.
'I must leave for my appointment.'

'You never said where you were going,' Izzy
dared to remark.

'A business appointment,' Rafiq lied, because
the instant he mentioned the Zenara research facility he was officially opening at the university he
too had attended, the game of secrecy and discretion would be blown to the four winds. And once
she knew that he was who he was—Zenarian roy-
alty—it might change her, might change the way
she behaved and the way she treated him, and he
already knew that he didn't want that to happen.

Springing upright, Rafiq gazed down at her
with a flare of scorching gold brightening his eyes
as his scrutiny rested a second too long on her full
pink lower lip and his imagination went crazy.
Long brown fingers clenched hard on the back of
the chair he had sat on because it was that much of
a challenge not to reach for her and drag her into
his arms. But it was too soon for that, way too soon
when she wasn't even flirting with him yet. And
if she didn't flirt, what then? It dawned on Rafiq
then that he was too habituated to sure-fire hook-

ups in very definite hook-up places and that for the first time he was trying something distinctly different. The realisation unnerved him just a little, for his entire experience of women outside marriage came down to eighteen months and a handful of one-night stands…

'This evening,' he breathed huskily, fighting off those uncharacteristic doubts, 'you will make dinner for us both and you will join me for the meal.'

Her smooth pale brow furrowed. 'Are you sure you want that?'

'Yes,' Rafiq delivered without hesitation. 'I would enjoy your company.'

Rafiq departed with his guards and Izzy continued to operate on automatic pilot by immediately abandoning the messy kitchen to complete the cleaning tasks she had still to accomplish. She changed the beds, cleaned the en suite bathroom and pulled out the vacuum cleaner and all the time she was fighting off constant feelings about Rafiq's invitation. It *wasn't* a date, it was just what he had called it, 'company', she told herself repressively, a totally casual arrangement. Even so, that still meant that he *had* to be interested in her to some degree, she reasoned. She glanced down at her worn jeans and tee. Did she want to eat with him looking so very obviously shabby? Even so, she didn't intend to get all dressed up and trowel on the make-up either lest she look madly keen. But, hey, there was nothing wrong with tarting herself up a little…

Izzy walked home at speed to the flat she shared with Maya and rifled frantically through her slender wardrobe before extending her search to her twin's. Some of Maya's stuff fitted her, even though Maya was taller and thinner. And it was one of her sister's dresses that she ended up choosing to wear. After washing her hair in the fastest shower on record, she put on the dress. It was green, stretchy and it hugged her curves but it was rather too long; however, it was the best option she had. At least it wasn't glittery or too short or too low-necked, which would give her the look of a woman who was trying too hard to impress, she reflected ruefully.

Even if she *was* trying the hardest she knew how to impress, a little voice prompted in the back of her head. She reddened as she added a little subtle cosmetic enhancement and crammed her feet into a pair of her sister's shoes. For dinner with a guy *that* hot, it was normal to make a big effort, she told herself forgivingly.

On the way back to the apartment she was forced to go shopping for the meal. She regretted her reluctance to buy the ingredients earlier because she didn't have much in her bank account and that reality shrank the range of meals that she could cook. Having settled on a Thai curry, she utilised the pass key she had yet to return and walked into the kitchen.

She had only been there about five minutes before Rafiq strolled in with a bottle of wine in his hand as if he had been awaiting her arrival, which bucked up her self-esteem no end. 'How was your afternoon?' he enquired lazily.

And she thought, God bless him, he doesn't have a clue. It didn't even cross his mind that she had spent the majority of his absence cleaning the apartment. Izzy simply smiled forgivingly, recognising that he came from a vastly different level of daily life from her own and she was tickled by that revealing question. 'Nothing special,' she said quietly, choosing not to embarrass him with an honest response.

'Let us hope this evening will be different,' he murmured almost awkwardly, settling the wine down on the counter right in her way where she was dicing vegetables. 'Where are the glasses?'

Yes, totally clueless, she thought with even stronger amusement, like a guy who had never been in a kitchen in his life. Rafiq was not accustomed to a woman cooking for him and even less accustomed to the working requirements of a kitchen in the midst of the preparation of a meal. She reached into the china cabinet to withdraw wine glasses and set them out for him while trying not to stare at him, because he had dressed down for the occasion. The formal business suit that had fitted him with designer-tailored perfection was gone, replaced with form-fitting denim jeans and a black shirt open at the neck. He still looked amazing. She reckoned he could even have rocked a dustbin bag with that lithe and powerful physique of his and those startling, stunning good looks. She no longer marvelled at her own susceptibility, reckoning that no man would ever provide her with so much temptation. Rafiq was in a class of his own: he was unique.

He poured a foaming golden liquid into the glasses and she squinted at the label on the bottle and her brows flew up. Champagne, the very best! She felt out of her element, watching him out of the corner of her eye as he lounged up against the hob where she was trying to cook, and almost groaned, recognising that she was dealing with a guy who was acting as if he had never been in a working kitchen in his life. It was weirdly cute, him striving to look cool and relaxed when the tension in his stance revealed that he was anything but relaxed and she took pity on him.

'Why don't you go and sit down next door while I finish up here?' Izzy suggested gently as she lifted her glass and sipped.

Rafiq's wide sensual mouth compressed, a muscle tightening in his strong jaw line. 'If that is what you want…but it doesn't seem very sociable to leave you alone.'

'It's fine,' Izzy murmured soothingly, wanting to smooth away the frown etched between his brows. 'I'll only be a few minutes.'

'You look amazing in that dress,' Rafiq breathed thickly, scanning her shapely figure with a hungry intensity that she could feel.

For an instant that appraisal unnerved her and then that anxious feeling evaporated. Only a few weeks earlier she and her twin had talked about whether or not they were too choosy about men and how uncomfortable, immature and secretive it felt to be the only virgins they knew. They had decided that they were too fussy, too busy holding onto something that that they had got tired of holding onto while everyone else their age moved on into another, seemingly more adult phase of life. When they were teenagers, they had assumed that Mr Perfect would come along, Mr Right, but now they were no longer so naïve about the society they lived in. The men they met weren't looking for sexual innocence and wouldn't place any value on it and as a result both of them had reached the conclusion that their restraint was pointless.

After all, even their mother hadn't waited until she was married. Lucia had been very honest about her life experience, freely admitting that she had got to twenty-five years of age zealously conserving what her traditional parents had assured her she had to conserve. But she had tired of respecting the social belief that to be valued she had to remain 'pure' even though the men she met were far from pure and, having fallen head over heels for their father, she had never lived to regret that decision, in spite of her judgemental family's shocked rejection of her.

So, when Rafiq shot her an all-encompassing look that almost ate her alive, Izzy went pink with awareness but, on another level, she thought, yes, I *could* with *him*, and she felt positively wicked and forward and shameless, but she couldn't help the heat that mushroomed up through her quivering body, because the desire that he was unafraid to show was coursing through her as well. And why should she be afraid of showing it? Of feeling that way? He made her body come alive in a way it never had before. He made her want what she had never wanted before. And who knew how long it would be before she met another man who had that effect on her?

Striving to act as cool as she knew how while struggling to handle all the different responses assailing her, Izzy set out the simple starter on the table and they sat down. 'So, how did your appointment go?' she enquired casually.

Rafiq shrugged a broad shoulder in dismissal. 'Nothing unusual. I would prefer to talk about you. Tell me about yourself…'

In a few words, she described her family. He asked about her brother, Matt.

'Was he born disabled?' he asked with a frown.

'No, he fell off a ladder when he was very young and broke his spine. He's paralysed from the waist down. He's eleven now and because he's been in the wheelchair for so long he bears it very well,' Izzy told him with quiet pride. 'But caring for him is tough on my parents so Maya and I help as much as we can. Hopefully I'll be able to do more when I can finally start full-time work.'

'That will be soon?' Rafiq assumed.

'Well, no, if everything goes according to plan, and I get a good enough pass in my degree, I'll have a year's teaching training course to do next,'

Izzy explained. 'I want to be a primary school teacher. Maya will probably take a high-flying job in the city. She's very good with numbers.'

Of course, she wasn't about to tell him the embarrassing truth that their parents were almost drowning in the amount of debt they had accrued over the years and at risk of losing their home, which had been specially adapted for her little brother's needs. All their choices always seemed to come down to money, which was mortifying, but Izzy felt sorriest of all for her sister because Maya had no desire to be a high-flyer in the stock market but since that kind of work paid the best, she would have to take it. At least Izzy, being the less academic twin, would be able to follow the career she wanted.

'Where are your guards?' she asked curiously, keen to get off the topic of future plans when she couldn't tell him the truth.

An almost imperceptible hint of colour honed the high cheekbones that lent Rafiq's lean dark features such powerful impact. The four guards hired at his uncle's insistence had been banished from the apartment while the remaining pair, who had long been in Rafiq's employment, were enjoying a night off that they would never mention to anyone. It outraged his pride that even as a fully grown adult male he was obliged to utilise such ploys to escape the intrusive nature of his security arrangements. 'They're off duty tonight because I'm not going out.'

'Tell me about Zenara,' Izzy suggested.

'Even though you've never heard of my country before?' Rafiq murmured with a touch of a raw edge to his intonation.

Izzy went pink and then lifted her chin at an angle. 'I offended you, didn't I?'

'Of course not,' Rafiq countered, noting how that extra colour in her cheeks merely brightened the sapphire blue of her eyes.

'Yes, I did. Well, I'm sorry, but we all have moments of ignorance,' she pointed out in her own defence. 'I expect I could come up with a topic that would leave you floundering too…if I *tried*.'

'Not in basic geography,' Rafiq told her drily.

Izzy compressed her soft pink mouth and shifted a narrow shoulder. 'Yeah, bet you could have completed the science paper I tanked on this morning too. I'm not gifted at science or general knowledge.'

Rafiq frowned. 'I thought you were studying for a degree in English?'

'To complete my degree I had to study a couple of different topics this year and everybody said the basic science course was easy-peasy.' Izzy's lip curled at the memory. 'Well, Maya could probably have aced it at five years old but even after swotting hard I couldn't answer some of the questions.'

'Hopefully you managed to answer enough to gain a pass,' Rafiq said encouragingly. 'It's a mistake to do a major post-mortem after an exam. People tend to underestimate their own performance unless they're exceptionally confident in their abilities. And by the sound of it you have been overshadowed your whole life by a very clever sister, which must have been difficult.'

'No, it wasn't!' Izzy protested defensively as she rose to fetch the main course. 'I was never envious of Maya. She always tried to help me whenever she could.'

Rafiq registered that he had entered a conversational minefield. 'We'll talk about Zenara instead,' he informed her, disconcerting her by that total change of subject.

In the wake of her protest, Izzy had paled, her innate honesty tugging at her conscience. 'No, what you said was right, although I never envied her,' she admitted reluctantly as she reappeared from the kitchen. 'Sometimes it *was* difficult being Maya's twin because people would make comparisons and have expectations that I could never meet.

But I love her, and I would never admit that to her. It wasn't her fault.'

'Of course, it wasn't. I have a teenaged brother and I am equally protective of him,' Rafiq confided.

Set at ease again, Izzy smiled at him, appreciating his insight and intelligence. His glorious black-lashed dark eyes shimmered like gold ingots in the subdued lighting and butterflies leapt and soared in her tummy, so that she felt almost intoxicated even on a glass and a half of champagne. 'Nothing's more important than family,' she remarked.

Studying her animated face and the smile that illuminated her porcelain-perfect skin, Rafiq gritted his even white teeth because she *still* wasn't flirting with him and he didn't know how the conversation had become so serious, as though they were on a date or something. And how would he know what *that* was like when he'd never been on a date in his life? But when he looked at her, let his attention linger on those big sparkling blue eyes, that wickedly luscious pink mouth full of promise, the delicate little slice of pale skin below her collarbone where a tiny pulse was beating, he burned for her as he had never burned for a woman, the hardness at his groin a constant nagging ache. He wanted to plunge his fingers into that amazing curly hair the glittering peachy colour of a desert dawn.

'You were going to tell me about your home country,' Izzy reminded him.

Rafiq pushed his plate away because they had finished eating.

'My goodness, I'm so busy talking I'm forgetting about the dessert course!' Izzy exclaimed, leaping out of her chair and vanishing into the kitchen.

Rafiq didn't want dessert. He wondered what would happen if he simply walked into the kitchen, snatched her up into his arms and carried her into his bedroom. She could thump him, she could say *no*. Right at that instant, he felt he could handle either negative reaction better than he could handle being passive when he was much more an aggressive, action-orientated kind of guy. He had been raised to take charge, to steer negotiations and wasn't sex a form of negotiation? An exchange in which both partners knew the score? She could not have come to the apartment to be alone with him for the meal and have expected any other kind of conclusion…could she? How the hell did he know?

In a blaze of frustration, Rafiq stared at her, catching the glow of awareness in her eyes as she looked back at him. He thrust back his chair and sprang upright. Izzy emerged from the kitchen again carrying bowls of fruit or something. His innate good manners warred with his lust and that seething hunger won hands down, sweeping away every other consideration. As she set down the bowls he stalked around the table and hauled her entire body up into his arms, the pleasure of finally touching her engulfing him in a heady surge.

Izzy blinked and gasped in complete shock. One minute her feet were on the ground and the next she was airborne, and he was kissing her.

'I am only hungry for you now,' Rafiq husked in a ragged undertone as her tiny frame quivered in his arms, huge sapphire eyes now locked to him with an appreciation he could no longer misinterpret.

After that explosive kiss, Izzy's heart was pounding so hard inside her chest she couldn't get breath into her lungs, and while on one level she felt that pouncing on her like a panther and lifting her off her feet wasn't quite what she had expected, on another secret level she was thrilled by the glow of wildness in his smouldering gaze and that urgent mouth on hers. It was so exciting, the most exciting thing that had *ever* happened to her and wasn't that sad, she chided herself, at her age? And

Rafiq was *that* hungry for *her*? That was a thrilling assurance for a young woman who had never seemed to inspire passion of that strength in any presentable man before. And he wasn't just presentable, he was downright drop-dead gorgeous…

CHAPTER THREE

RAFIQ CARRIED IZZY into the bedroom and laid her down with great care on the bed.

'This…it is what you want too?' he was careful to check.

Izzy sat back against the leather headboard, still a little stunned by the speed and mode of her arrival into a more intimate setting. Rafiq was being very direct and of course she understood why it had to be that way. No man could risk a misunderstanding in such a scenario. Even so, colour ran up her face like a banner because the decision she had acknowledged earlier in the kitchen still felt so new and fresh to her; she would sleep with him, finally discover what sex was all about, only, if she was honest, she hadn't really expected it to happen so fast between them.

'Yes…this is what I want too,' she almost whispered, ramming down all her insecurities with ferocious determination because she was convinced that a wildly desirable opportunity with someone like Rafiq was only likely to happen once in her lifetime and she wasn't planning to squander it. 'But I'm a little shy, not very experienced,' she added in cautious warning, in case his hopes were focused on more erotic thrills than she was likely to deliver.

Suddenly, Rafiq felt as though he could finally breathe again. The idea of her walking away, turning her back and rejecting him had been a fear strong enough to freeze him in his tracks because there was something about her, presumably a very *sexy* something, that totally set him on fire with lust. He wondered if it was those huge blue eyes or possibly that ripe pink mouth or even the crazy copper curls surrounding that triangular face. Perhaps even the reality that shy didn't turn him off, as her face said she feared, it actually turned him on *more*. Indeed, it meant that he was much less likely to be taken by surprise by anything *she* did.

'That doesn't bother me,' he admitted, hitting the buttons to close the blinds on the window and dim the lights even though, by choice, he would have put her under a spotlight, but her comfort, her ability to relax with him, were more important. He kicked off his shoes and vaulted onto the bed beside her. She startled and his flashing smile tilted his shapely mouth again, his hand coming up to frame her face as he lowered his head and tasted her mouth again with all the urgent demand he was struggling to hold back.

Izzy travelled from nervous tension back into a paradise where everything seemed to be about just one perfect kiss because he was one hell of a kisser. In that line, she was plenty experienced, even though no man had ever kissed her and made her very toes curl until Rafiq. It was as if he lit a spark somewhere down deep inside her, a spark that fostered a spread of warmth in her pelvis and made her thighs tighten. Her whole body turned liquid, her breasts swelling inside her bra, the peaks tightening and pushing against the lace.

His lean, long-fingered hands roamed slowly over her, cupping, touching, moulding, and she quivered, heat roaring through her in an almost unmanageable surge. Her hands lifted and found his wide shoulders to explore and then the long sweep of his back, the literal heat of him burning through the silk of his shirt.

'Take it off,' he told her.

Izzy went for the buttons, unwilling to break the kissing to look, and she must have been too slow at the task because with an earthy groan he pulled back from her and just ripped off the shirt, buttons flying everywhere.

'I guess you don't value your clothes very much,' she muttered helplessly.

'Not when they get in the way of what I want, which is your hands on me,' Rafiq growled, taking that moment to reach down for the hem of her dress and lift it up and over her head.

Disconcerted to find herself so swiftly reduced to her bra and panties, Izzy tensed, lacking the confidence in her body that was required to feel calm beneath his smouldering dark golden gaze.

'You are *so* gorgeous,' Rafiq breathed raggedly. She glanced up at him in stark shock and it was there in his appreciative gaze that he truly believed that.

It wasn't quite enough encouragement for her to lie back and preen herself like Cleopatra on a ceremonial barge, but it certainly made a difference to the way she generally viewed herself as the *plain* twin. After all, it had been said within her hearing many times when she was a child because people weren't careful about making such statements around her, and it was a role she had unconsciously accepted and assumed to be the truth.

Empowered by Rafiq's statement, however, Izzy went back to taste that wickedly sensual mouth of his for herself and he reacted with flattering enthusiasm, pressing her back against the pillows and kissing her breathless, lean fingers sliding beneath her to release her bra in what she believed to be the smoothest move ever. And then he was curving his big hands to the swell of her full pale breasts, touching, smoothing, rolling and squeezing her achingly sensitive nipples, sending piercing shards of pleasure travelling straight to her groin.

As he drove a thigh between her legs, pushing against the most sensitive spot of all, her entire body jackknifed upward, a muffled cry wrenched from her throat as the excitement rippling through her rose in a blinding, stabbing wave. His mouth travelled down the slope of her neck, kissing a path down to the erect buds, dallying there with lips and tongue and teeth until the breath was sobbing between her lips, and he crushed her mouth under his again, his tongue delving deep, twining with hers, only partially answering the desperate, fevered craving controlling her.

'You want me...' Rafiq savoured with satisfaction.

'Wouldn't be here if I didn't,' she gasped, lost in those dark dramatic eyes gleaming with sparks of gold in the low light, marvelling that he felt the need to state the obvious, because who wouldn't

want him? His eyes were absolutely beautiful—
all of him was absolutely beautiful, she acknowledged dizzily as he snaked his hips back from her
to unzip his jeans and take them off, the generous
bulge thrusting against his boxer briefs making her
stare for a split second. He looked a little larger
than she had been counting on, she conceded, but
Mother Nature had fashioned men and women to
fit, so there wasn't likely to be a problem in that
line, she told herself.

His sensual lips sought hers again as he whisked
off her panties, pulling her onto his thighs as he
threw back the duvet and settled her on the sheet.
He gazed down at her with wondering thankful-
ness because she was full of passion just like him
and it wasn't an act to impress him or even a ruse
to take a photo of him, making him the boastful
virtual equivalent of a show-and-tell. He smoothed
hungrily grateful hands over her, his very *last sin*,
and she was perfect, a perfect doll as she lay there
looking up at him with those wide-open cerulean-
blue eyes, as clear as the Zenarian sky in summer,
against her pale redhead's skin. He threaded long
fingers through her wonderfully soft, silky ring-
lets and shifted down the bed to tug her to him and
crush her luscious mouth under his again.

His hands wandering over her curvy bottom,

pulling her to him, he rejoiced in her softness and smoothness and responsiveness as he slid down the bed to spread her thighs and assure that she got as much pleasure out of the encounter as he expected to. Startled by that move, scolding herself as the most appalling wave of awkward embarrassment washed over her, Izzy threw her head back on the pillows and closed her eyes tight. If she didn't see what he was doing, it would be more bearable, more difficult to recall that he was looking at her...*there*.

Yet that first lick from his tongue over her feminine core sent a wave of heat shooting through her as hot as a lava flow and every nerve ending she possessed screamed into immediate response. Nothing had ever felt that good, nothing had ever felt so necessary to her that if he had stopped, she would have screamed even louder in frustration.

Involuntarily one of her hands closed into his black hair and it was like thick silk between her fingers, and those eyes of his when he looked at her, yes, somehow her own eyes had opened, well, it was somehow the sexiest thing ever. Her extreme self-consciousness died away because she knew she wanted him more than she had ever wanted anything and that there was nothing wrong with feeling how she was feeling. And finally, she relaxed, although possibly relaxed wasn't the right word to describe how exquisite sensation sent her a little crazy and out of control.

Her body took over without her volition, her hips rising in tune with a racy beat that was new to her, little shudders of reaction tingling through her from her pelvis. The shudders increased to a level of devastating pressure that tightened and tightened around her womb until she thought she would go insane. The ferocious need that clawed at her was unbearable and it tore breathless little whimpers from her throat until finally she reached a peak and it felt as though she were internally combusting with pleasure from the outside in, rippling pulsations of sheer delight shooting through her to leave her limp and no longer on what seemed to be the same planet. The total experience was infinitely more sensational then she had expected.

That was fortunate, she soon learned, because as Rafiq came over her—having reached for protection, she noted with relief—what followed was not quite so enjoyable. She went from pliable to stiff as he nudged at her damp centre, easing in. As he groaned with apparent satisfaction at how tight he said she was, Izzy was concentrating on the newness of sensation, and then he tilted up her hips and thrust deep and it hurt. She hadn't been expecting an actual pain, had assumed there would possibly be a sting or a faint twinge of discomfort but not anything that truly hurt, and she cried out at the pain of it.

And everything stopped: *he* froze, *she* froze.

'It was my first time,' she heard herself gabble in mortification. 'Maybe I should've mentioned it but it's done, so let's finish.'

'I don't think so,' Rafiq growled, thrown into a loop by the unwelcome news that he had bedded a virgin, which to him meant that he had taken advantage of someone more vulnerable, more innocent, in short a woman he should never have touched.

Unexpectedly, Izzy found that she was amused because in the blink of an eye Rafiq had transformed from passionate lover into a naked masculine pillar of censorious disapproval, the gorgeous eyes angry, the strong jaw line clenched, the sensual mouth flattened. 'It's not your choice, it was mine and it's a little late to be a party pooper,' she told him staunchly, absolutely refusing to be embarrassed after what they had already shared.

'Izzy…' Rafiq began, astonished to see the sparkle of laughter in her sapphire gaze and disconcerted yet again by her.

Izzy tilted back her hips and wrapped her legs

round his hips. She didn't have very long legs, so it was a struggle to execute that imprisoning gesture that told him what she didn't have the words to tell him because she really didn't understand herself at that moment either. But he wasn't going anywhere, not until he had finished. 'Well, see if you can fight your way free,' she urged with a helpless giggle.

And Rafiq's ready sense of humour came to the rescue because it was a ridiculous suggestion when she was so tiny and he was so much bigger. Involuntarily, he smiled and she rested her fingers against his softened lips and murmured, 'That's better. It's not your fault it hurt, not your fault you're over-endowed.'

It was involuntary again but Rafiq laughed. 'And how would you know whether I am or not?'

'I'm assuming that's why it hurt, because you weren't rough,' she said very softly.

Something about that tone, or possibly it was the worryingly anxious plea in her bright blue gaze, shot every other thought out of his mind. He angled back his tousled dark head and contrived, with admitted difficulty because of the difference in their heights and their still thoroughly joined bodies, to kiss her, the fierce tension draining out of his lean, powerful body as though it had never been.

He had never wanted anything as much as he

had wanted her and now it seemed a cruelly appropriate punishment for his conscience that he had taken a virgin as his last sin. Defying that punitive thought, he stamped it down and shifted his lean hips, revelling in the feel of her, the ache at his groin climbing with every tiny movement she made. The hunger and the need burned like a fierce flame through him and he couldn't resist her. At least that was what he told himself: that she was more temptation than any normal man could be expected to withstand. Only on another level, he knew he wasn't a normal man, that he was supposed to be stronger, tougher, harder: the guy raised and expected to always do the right thing.

But *still* he didn't do it. He surrendered to the overpowering hunger, driving into her again with caution but also with deep physical satisfaction, delighting in the way her eyes clouded over again and her heart-shaped face relaxed to reveal pleasure. Never had he needed so badly to give a woman pleasure and even though the lust riding him was brutally strong, he took his time, measured his pace, watched her for every tiny sign of response.

The heat in her lower body rose again, the flood of excitement unleashing as her heart hammered so fast inside her chest she could barely breathe. Izzy felt ridiculously happy and didn't know why.

Because he had listened to her? Because she had got him out of that grim mood that had promised to wreck everything and transform her adult decision into a big messy mistake to be regretted? She didn't know—knew only that she had accidentally discovered that her 'bathroom guy', as he would be in her brain for ever, had an unexpectedly *very* serious side to his nature.

Something deep inside her quickened and her body clenched around him as little tremors of blissful excitement mounted. His every movement became all important, stoking the pulses of hot sensation in her pelvis until the fire rose again, throwing her on a wild cry of pleasure into climax again, and she fell back against the pillows, her hand smoothing over the long, damp, satin smoothness of his flexing spine.

'That was amazing,' Rafiq said breathlessly, pulling back from her to flop back on the bed beside her, leaving her feeling strangely abandoned.

Lighten up, Izzy, she urged herself ruefully. Stop piling silly expectations on him and then feeling sad when he doesn't deliver. Nobody had asked *him* if he wanted to play a leading part in her most romantic fantasies, the fantasies that until that moment she would've said were more her twin's department than her own. Striving to act casual, she watched him vault out of the bed and head into the bathroom, belatedly appreciating that he was disposing of the contraception and marvelling that she had forgotten that practical aspect in favour of wishing for a hug. They were still essentially strangers, she reminded herself doggedly. Maybe hugging was too much too soon…

In the bathroom, his thoughts very far removed from the subtleties of sexual aftercare, Rafiq was wrestling with his essential streak of honesty. He *should* tell her…but why? Nothing could come of the accident but still…

Rafiq came to a halt in the doorway.

Izzy contemplated him with a helpless smile. There he was, tall and bronzed and naked and beautiful and he had given her a lot of pleasure. She had definitely made the *right* decision.

'The condom split,' Rafiq admitted flatly. 'But there is no risk involved for you. I have never had unprotected sex and I cannot father children.'

Izzy was shocked by the sheer size of that admission and the hard, shuttered look on his lean, darkly beautiful features as he made it. 'How do you know you can't father children?' she couldn't help asking.

'Because I was married for a long time and it

didn't happen,' he confided tautly. 'So, no risk involved for you in that field.'

End of discussion, she recognised, shaken that he had been married for what he deemed a long time when he was still seemingly so young. 'How old are you?' she prompted helplessly.

'Twenty-eight.'

So a very youthful marriage that had presumably ended in divorce—not her business, she had to remind herself when other questions threatened to brim from her lips, and she swallowed them back hard to reassure him with her information.

'I'm on the pill,' she told him quietly.

Rafiq frowned in surprise. 'But…why?'

Hugging the sheet, Izzy sat up, copper corkscrew curls springing up like a halo around her flushed face. She wasn't prepared to tell him the whole truth, not when it revolved around her mother. 'My sister and I know someone who had an unplanned pregnancy and we never wanted it to happen to us that way, so we chose instead to be prepared for all eventualities.'

'Are you staying?' Rafiq enquired, ignoring the explanation that only emphasised to him that they lived in very different worlds, he in a world where pregnancy would have been an unashamed joy but she in one where it would have been an apparent punishment of some kind.

Just being asked that question freaked Izzy out. In ten seconds, she was out of the bed and gathering up her clothes at the speed of a fleeing squirrel.

'I was hoping you would stay,' Rafiq rephrased, accepting that he had been clumsy. 'But I have to leave very early in the morning and would likely be gone by the time you awake.'

'Leaving the UK?' Izzy queried tightly, without warning feeling as though he had buried an axe between her shoulder blades.

'Yes…'

Izzy slid past him into the bathroom and shut the door. He knocked on it and with reluctance she opened the door a crack.

'I don't want us to be so brief…but I don't have a choice.'

'Why? *Why* don't you have a choice?' Izzy pressed in desperation.

His ridiculously long black lashes shielded his stunning gaze. 'I can't explain that.'

'You know what? That's fine. I'm going to have a shower and go home,' Izzy told him with quiet dignity even though her stomach was already in the mood to heave.

It was *over*. In fact, it had been virtually over even before it had got to begin, she reckoned, stricken. She had dimly assumed that she was on a date when in reality she had been succumbing to a one-night stand and that made her feel very, *very* stupid and naïve. She hadn't realised that he was only in Oxford for one night and that tomorrow she would be receiving a text from the cleaning agency to do the changeover clean again. Best not to be in the apartment alone when that text came, she reasoned dully, as no doubt sleeping with the client was yet another fireable offence.

Dear heaven, how had she contrived to be so dumb? How had she managed to decide to sleep with him and somehow idealise the decision into something it wasn't and could never be? And she had *believed* that, of the two of them, Maya was the romantic dreamer?

Showered and dressed, Izzy emerged from the bathroom in record time.

Back in his jeans but barefoot, Rafiq extended the handbag she had left behind in the lounge, proving that he was surprisingly at home with a woman's needs. The gesture only increased her suspicions. 'Are you sure you're not still married?' she demanded thinly.

'I am not married but—' Rafiq breathed in deep, like a male mustering his strength '—I will be married again some time soon.'

'You bastard…you're engaged and you slept with *me*?' Izzy exclaimed and she hit his shoulder with her handbag as she swung it like a weapon.

Rafiq said nothing because there was nothing he could say without revealing his true identity. Being struck by someone for the first time ever shocked him, but not enough for him to rebuke her because the evening had turned into an irrefutable disaster and he didn't blame her for the way she felt. He was rigid as he extended an envelope to her.

'What's this?' she questioned.

'The money I promised you,' Rafiq advanced warily. 'I pay my debts.'

'I don't want the money now!' Izzy framed shakily, her face very white. 'Not after what we've just done!'

In a sudden movement, Rafiq snatched the bag out of her nerveless hand, opened it and dug the envelope into it before handing it back to her.

'You do realise that this is the last straw…the biggest insult?' Izzy shouted at him, stricken. 'You're paying me off like I'm a hooker or something!'

'We both know that it was not like that between us,' Rafiq framed in a raw undertone.

'But that's what it *feels* like now!' Izzy slung back at him as she stalked out of the bedroom, out of the apartment and back to her own life with the knowledge that she should never have strayed from what she understood and what was familiar because, without those guidelines and boundaries, it was easy to get badly hurt.

And she *was* hurt. On the way home she took her daily contraceptive pill from her handbag where she kept them, not wishing to trust in the convictions of the guy who had already let her down. But it had been *her* hopes he'd disappointed. He hadn't promised anything, hadn't broken her heart with lies either. He was engaged though, had been unfaithful to some other woman with her, which made her feel soiled, tainted by association. That wounded like another knife twisting inside her…how could it not? That took her right back to basics and she wasn't the slightest bit surprised that, when she got back to the apartment, she was horribly sick on her empty stomach and never had she been more grateful that her sister was not around to see her at her lowest ebb.

CHAPTER FOUR

Maya returned from her visit home and stayed in the bedroom most of the evening, clearly in no mood to chat, and Izzy was grateful, if not discomfited, by her twin's preoccupation.

'How's stuff at home?' she asked over breakfast the following morning.

Maya grimaced. 'The usual mess and Dad saying that everything's going to be all right even though there's no way it will be.'

'Dad doesn't change.' Izzy sighed. 'How's Mum?'

'Keeping faith in Dad as usual,' her sister said wearily.

'So, what do we do?'

'Anything we can do,' Maya breathed tautly. 'And that's not a lot at the moment.'

Izzy hugged her own misery to herself in silence because Maya had quite enough to be contending with at present and Izzy had no plans to add to her burden. Undoubtedly her sister would share once life had lightened up a little, she thought tiredly, while still wondering how someone like Rafiq, whom she had only known for less than twenty-four stupid hours, could dent her usually cheerful nature to the extent that she felt as though an armoured tank had run over her. Even so, there was no point beating herself up continually over events she had no power to change, most especially when she was in the midst of her final exams, she reminded herself squarely.

Over the subsequent month, Izzy swotted hard and sat exam after exam, worrying every step of the way and then discovering a different and an entirely more frightening possibility dawning on her when her period was two weeks late. Could Rafiq have lied to her about being infertile? Well, he hadn't been decent enough to mention that he was engaged, had he? By that stage, Izzy was willing to believe any evil of Rafiq. He had left her two thousand pounds in that envelope for cooking two meals for him and presumably, whether he was prepared to admit the offensive fact or not, for being a willing bed partner. He had treated her exactly like a hooker, thrusting cash at her as she departed, and her blood still boiled over that truth. But she didn't understand either how she could possibly have conceived while she was taking the pill; she hadn't missed one…had she?

The ice queen of a doctor at the student health centre soon disabused her of that conviction with the reminder that she had been on a course of antibiotics for a mild infection only a couple of weeks earlier and that it was stated quite clearly on the leaflet that came with the pills that antibiotics could interfere with birth-control medication and that in that situation extra precautions should be taken.

'Yes…but who reads those leaflets?' Izzy had mumbled while the lady doctor looked at her as though she was an idiot when she already felt like one.

It was too late but, devastated by the confirmation that, yes, she was indeed pregnant, Izzy read that stupid leaflet on the bus on the way home and learned that even that episode of sickness she had had that night after leaving Rafiq would have lessened the effectiveness of her birth-control pills. It seemed to her that every piece of happenstance bad luck she could have had had all visited her on one day but she blamed Rafiq most of all for that lie about infertility, for parting from her without even giving her his surname or any means of contacting him. *Of course, an engaged man wouldn't want any comeback from his one-night stand, would he?* she thought nastily. And why should he get to walk away from her pregnancy when she *couldn't*?

There was another side of the coin to Izzy's feelings about her pregnancy. She adored babies, had always hoped that there would be children in her future *but…*?

At that precise moment in her life, a pregnancy was nothing short of a disaster, she acknowledged unhappily. She needed to be able to complete her education with a teaching qualification to earn a decent living and how was a baby going to factor into that? And what about the costs involved in raising a child? Everyone knew that babies, sweet and wondrous as they were, cost a fortune to bring up!

The more Izzy thought about what Rafiq had done to her, the angrier she became, because he had walked away afterwards, deliberately ensuring that she had no chance of identifying him or contacting him for support or anything else.

She accepted that a sneakier approach to her dilemma was required. Determined to identify Rafiq, Izzy called in at the rental agency that managed the penthouse apartment she cleaned and got into a cosy chat with the receptionist. In tones of wonder, she described the absolutely gorgeous guy with his bodyguards whom she had supposedly seen when leaving the building.

'That must've been the Prince…' The receptionist sighed, hanging on her every word. 'I never saw him, of course. People that important don't make their own bookings but when his staff contacted us on his behalf, I looked him up on the website because I was curious…a prince, you know, and he *is* very, very good-looking, isn't he? I wish I'd seen him in the flesh.'

'The Prince?' Izzy repeated chokily. 'Like a *real* prince?'

'Heir to the Zenarian throne. It's all on their website,' her companion told her abstractedly. 'He's something special.'

Izzy was gobsmacked. A *prince*? A freakin' prince? And now she understood the bodyguards, the air of imperious expectation, the cash, the reluctance to tell her anything about himself, which she had only registered afterwards, when it was far too late to see that attitude as suspicious. She raced home purely to look up the website that had been mentioned and, true enough, there Rafiq was in a photo along with his uncle, the Regent, the heir to the blasted throne of the whole country!

Even worse, there was a very small reference to a rumour that the heir could be getting married again soon.

Breathing heavily, Izzy paced the room, relieved that once again her twin was back in London with their parents, attending job interviews. Sooner or later she would have to come clean about her problems but, right now, Maya had more than enough on her plate and Izzy was determined not to lean on her sister as well. It was a wonder, she thought guiltily, that Maya hadn't already drowned with the sheer weight of them all clinging to her, constantly looking to her for advice and support.

No, on this occasion, Izzy would deal with her own issues and act like an adult. Not like the time she had been bullied at school. Not like the time Maya had rescued her from drowning in a winter river and almost drowned herself. Not like the time Izzy had broken her leg and Maya had sat up all night in hospital with her. No, just for once, Izzy would handle herself.

She would fly to Zenara using the money Rafiq had given her to cover the cost of the flight. She had to tell him that she was pregnant *before* he got married. That was only fair to him and the woman he was planning to marry. It would be mean to withhold such information until a later date. In any case, the child she carried was his baby as well, and, while he had a responsibility towards his fiancée, he also had a responsibility towards Izzy and his child. Rafiq would have to man up and handle the situation and that was *his* problem, *not* hers!

It cost a small fortune to book a flight to Zenara and, by the time she had booked and paid for a hotel for three nights as well, she didn't have enough money left to book a return flight. But she was quite sure that bathroom guy with his private jet and his reputed billions would ensure that she swiftly got home again, she thought bitterly. He would want her smuggled out of the country again where she couldn't cause His Royal Highness any further embarrassment!

Rafiq had *lied* to her, she reminded herself, because it wasn't like her to be bitter and angry but that was what the whole experience of Rafiq, his lies and evasions and an unexpected pregnancy had done to her. Instead of feeling able to rejoice in the baby she carried, she felt ashamed because love hadn't featured in that conception, not as it had in her parents' case. And Rafiq had hurt her pride and her heart, of course he had. She had been well on the way to tumbling into an infatuation with him. She hadn't realised that she wasn't on a level playing field. She hadn't even suspected that she could be dealing with a real VIP, a foreign royal, no doubt accustomed to taking his sexual pleasure where he found it even if it meant wining and dining a humble student cleaner to seduce her into bed!

Izzy couldn't understand what the problem was at the airport in Zenara. She had disembarked from the plane, shown her documentation and then somehow everything had gone wrong and, instead of being left free to go about her business, she had been ushered into a small office for an interview.

The heat was killing her, the small fan on the desk in front of her making little impression on her condition. Her cotton top and linen trousers were sticking to her perspiring flesh and her brow was damp.

An older man entered and gave her a small tight smile. 'Miss Campbell. I am sorry for this inconvenience,' he told her.

Izzy went limp with relief at finally meeting someone who could speak her language. 'I don't understand why I'm not being allowed to leave the airport.'

'We have certain entrance requirements for unaccompanied single women and I'm afraid you don't meet the regulations,' he told her.

Izzy tilted her chin, not in the mood for some silly form of bureaucracy after sitting trapped in that claustrophobic room for more than an hour. 'In what way?'

'You have not stated your business in Zenara.'

'I said I was a tourist,' Izzy protested.

'You have booked a hotel for only three nights and have not booked a return flight. Unfortunately, this sends up certain flags in our system. If you have any friends or connections in Zenara who could vouch for your character, please give me their details now and I will contact them.'

Izzy blinked. 'The only person I know in Zenara is Prince Rafiq…'

The silence of shock that fell then pleased her because she was so tired, so hungry and so darned hot that she was utterly miserable and all she wanted was out of the blasted airport into the air-conditioned cool of a hotel.

'And this…er…acquaintance?' the older man began very awkwardly, clearly not sure how best to proceed when it came to questioning someone with a possible link to the royal family.

Something in Izzy snapped then, something like the last link to her sanity, because she had just had enough and she breathed wearily, 'He is the father of my child.'

At that point the world around Izzy went crazy as cries of disbelief, shock and rapped-out exchanges in a foreign language broke out over her head. Overpowered by it all, she stood up because her back was aching and she was feeling queasy. An ocean of darkness instantly enfolded her, and she dropped without a sound into a dead faint. Pandemonium broke out while she was unconscious and rushed into an ambulance with a police escort.

Izzy surfaced back to consciousness in a bedroom so splendid that she was disorientated. Not a hospital, not a hotel either. Still fully clothed, only her shoes removed, she was lying on a grand four-poster bed with a trio of doctors standing at the foot of it, giving names that she instantly forgot while assuring her that she was in the safest of places because she was in the *royal palace*.

Frozen back against the pillows by that startling information, she blinked rapidly, wishing that she could think clearly and less like a zombie. Without warning, the bedroom door opened and heads started dipping in a show of respect and Rafiq strode in, the proud lineaments of his bronzed and flawless features inhumanly calm and collected for a single man who'd had a woman announce at the airport that he was the father of her child. The airport, for goodness' sake! Izzy could feel hot colour sweeping from her head to toes, her fury with Rafiq eclipsed entirely at that moment by the situation she was in. He had to think she was a madwoman but nothing that he might be thinking or feeling was showing on the surface.

Involuntarily, her attention lingered on him. The high cheekbones and strong hollows, the blade-straight black brows, the stunning deep-set eyes fringed by those outrageous thick lashes. Get over it, he's gorgeous, it's not relevant right now, she scolded herself anxiously as he sank down with fluid grace for so large a man in the chair by the bed and reached for her hand in a startlingly supportive gesture.

'How are you feeling?' Rafiq asked graciously, for all the world as though they had only parted as close friends in recent days, instead of the weeks that had passed since their last explosive meeting. Her fingers trembled in the light grasp of his.

'Groggy,' she muttered truthfully, gently removing her fingers from his hold while striving not to make a production out of the withdrawal. She was painfully aware that they were not alone, and she was keen to follow his example and behave as though everything between them were normal. 'Think I'm just tired…'

'You must rest, of course,' Rafiq murmured quietly. 'Beforehand, however, the doctors are asking if they could have your consent to carry out an ultrasound procedure…?'

In awe of his self-assurance, his ability to act as though there were nothing crazy about the situation, she nodded jerkily. 'Yes, that would be fine, I suppose. Though it might be too early to see much…'

He was sheathed like a rapier blade in a pale grey suit teamed with a white shirt and a red silk tie. Her eyes continually tracked a path back to him, connecting with scorching gold semi-screened by his black lashes, and in the depths of his steady gaze she caught the merest glimpse of all the strong emotion and reaction he was suppressing for the sake of appearances, she assumed. He was so strong, so self-disciplined, she recognised, uncomfortable with that moment of truth and deliberately turning her head away. What on earth had got into her at the airport to say such a thing? Inside herself, she cringed at her reckless impulsive revelation, recalling the astounded response she had drawn from her audience before she fainted.

An ultrasound machine was wheeled in for the scan. A nurse rolled up Izzy's cotton tunic top a few inches and Izzy lifted her hips to enable the stretchy waistband of her casual trousers to be rolled down a little, baring her still-flat stomach. The transponder ball rubbed over her exposed skin and goosebumps broke out on her skin as a galloping heartbeat began to thunder through the room and she gasped, peering in wonder at the screen the operator was indicating to her, breaking into a flood of words in her own language with a huge smile.

'T-twins...' Rafiq stammered in a hoarse undertone. 'You are carrying twins. It is too early as yet to know the gender, but the doctor believes that they are fraternal, not identical.'

His hand had found hers again, she didn't know when or how, was, indeed, in too much shock to notice anything beyond the screen where the operator was beaming and chattering away, outlining the two tiny vague bean shapes while their heartbeats went on thundering. Twins, she thought in wonderment, with an undernote of panic because her mother had shared what a challenge it had often been to raise two babies. And yet there they were, already part of her, she acknowledged, struggling to concentrate as Rafiq translated the information she was being given as well as the round after round of hearty congratulations delivered to them both as though they were a proper couple.

In the aftermath of all that excitement, Izzy felt drained and her head flopped back heavily on the pillow. Although their audience had melted away with the promise of pictures of the scan to be brought back later, Izzy was too exhausted to deal with Rafiq and all the many complications that their situation would unleash. Mercifully he seemed to understand that because he released her hand and stood up.

'You should rest now. We will talk later,' he murmured unevenly, something ragged in his voice that tugged at her, but her eyelids were too heavy to open and she drifted off to sleep on that last abstracted thought.

Rafiq had been plunged into a state of earth-shattering shock. In fact, he had to walk out of the palace into the ornamental garden that fronted it to deal with that shock because he didn't have the slightest doubt that, when Izzy had conceived within such a time frame, *he* was responsible. That far, he had innate trust in her. He was going to be a father. His bodyguards waited at the edge of the garden, watching Rafiq wander around the lavender-edged paths that traversed the tranquil stretch of green grass, maintained at such huge expense of water in the Zenarian heat. Throughout

that aimless wandering he was battling to adapt to
the idea that he could truly *have* a child of his own.

And it was an *enormous* shock because Rafiq
had long accepted that he was infertile, and that
fatherhood would never be an option for him. Yet,
one little contraceptive accident and Izzy had conceived. How likely was that? What had happened
to that birth control she had been taking?

But he genuinely didn't care. He was *so* grateful, so ecstatic that it *was* possible for him to father
a child that he could barely catch a breath. Such a
development lifted all the weighty responsibility
from his little brother's shoulders because Zayn
would no longer be expected to marry to provide an
heir to the Zenarian throne. Zayn would be left free
as Rafiq had once dreamt of being and, in being
free, he would set Rafiq free of guilt and concern.

In fact, Izzy's pregnancy totally changed everything Rafiq had once taken for granted. A child,
two children indeed, he recalled almost dizzily.
The palace staff had automatically assumed that
Izzy was his wife, married abroad, it being the
default position of a conservative culture to believe that a man of his background could only have
achieved parenthood within conventional boundaries.

But she *wasn't* his wife, this amazing woman

who had contrived to conceive his children. *Children*, he savoured, child in the plural. Nobody else could possibly understand what that single word meant to Rafiq, long accustomed to viewing himself as the inadequate husband who had denied his wife her basic, *desperate* need to have a child. It transformed his entire view of life in a way that only *he* could understand. He had to marry Izzy, as soon as it could possibly be arranged. There was no other choice.

But even as he came to terms with the wonderful change Izzy had brought to his life, stark fear underlined that new knowledge. As a boy, Rafiq had seen his mother die in the aftermath of his brother's birth. In the panic of rushing, fearful staff, struggling to deal with an emergency they were not medically equipped to handle, the presence of the quiet boy hovering at the back of the room had been overlooked. He remembered every moment of that experience and it had chilled him that the arrival of new life could bring death in its wake. Pregnancy and delivery could still be dangerous for a woman. Concern for Izzy gripped him, but it was not a concern he would share with her because the last thing a first-time expectant mother needed was a nervous partner even more fearful than she was.

* * *

'What time is it?' Izzy asked of the friendly female face that came into view as she lifted her head, registering that she felt truly rested for the first time in days. Of course, the stress she had been under meant that she hadn't been sleeping and hadn't been eating very sensibly either.

'Early evening, Your Royal Highness. Would you like a shower or a bath?' she was asked.

'I would love one and a change of clothes,' Izzy responded pleasantly, reluctant to enquire about that strange appellation. Why would anyone anywhere think that she was royal?

But even as she slid her legs slowly out of the bed, she remembered afresh that startling announcement of hers at the airport. It had erupted from her as panic took a hold. She had told them that Rafiq was the father of her child and she suspected that official label, that assumption that they could only be married if that were the case, was linked to that and she almost cringed in mortification, wondering what had come over her and why she had had to finally give way to her overload of stress in front of an audience. That was why she had been brought to the palace and a trio of doctors had arrived to attend to her. Airports and palaces, full of gossiping, chattering employees, were very public places. That was why Rafiq had felt constrained to act as though her arrival and everything that had happened since were normal. Move on by, nothing to stare at here, she paraphrased numbly.

The maid showed her into a reassuringly modern bathroom. Her suitcase already sat in readiness for her on a stand and she dug into it to extract a clean outfit and headed for the shower, stripping off her badly creased clothing and letting the garments fall to the floor. She freshened up in record time, keen to see Rafiq again and get things sorted out, say what she had to say while hopefully remaining civil if he planned to have a relationship with *their* children. That was the problem, she acknowledged ruefully—everything she said and did now would have repercussions that could impact on the happiness of the babies she carried. It would be unwise to be as unpleasant as she had originally intended. Yet, sadly, she was still so angry with him that just the thought of him enraged her.

Walking back into the bedroom to find a small table set with food by the window would have been most welcome, because she was really hungry, had Rafiq not been seated on the other side of the table awaiting her appearance. He flew upright, a very tall well-groomed and powerful figure in a designer suit that fitted his impressive physique to perfection. And then he made the very great mistake of smiling at her.

'Don't you dare smile at me, you…you creep!' Izzy launched at him in disbelief at that smile. 'You *lied* to me. You told me you couldn't father children! You are also engaged to another woman! I don't want to even think about how *she* feels about this mess!'

In the face of that attack, Rafiq breathed in deep and slow. She looked amazing, a glow in her pale cheeks, bright eyes like sapphire stars contrasting with those glossy copper curls that glinted in the sunlight. She wore a strappy vest top with trousers, a top that only hinted at the bounty of her lush breasts and the shadowy cleft between but that thought was all it took for his groin to tighten and the throb of arousal to set in.

'It was my genuine belief that I was infertile,' Rafiq murmured and he spread his lean brown hands in a graceful gesture that emphasised his acceptance of that conviction. 'Although nothing was ever found wrong with me or my wife, we were together for ten years and we were unable to conceive a child.'

'Ten years? You must've got married very young,' Izzy heard herself comment without having meant to.

'I was sixteen. Fadith was seventeen. We were far too young, but our guardians chose to believe otherwise,' Rafiq countered levelly.

'What happened to her? Are you divorced?' Izzy pressed.

'She caught a chest infection that turned into pneumonia and died. It happened very fast,' he clarified.

'I'm sorry...' Izzy whispered awkwardly, disconcerted by his explanation.

'Come and sit down now and have something to eat...'

'I have a lot to shout at you about,' Izzy argued, struggling to recapture her nerve.

'You can shout after you have eaten,' Rafiq pointed out smoothly. 'I promise not to deprive you of the opportunity.'

A laugh almost bubbled out of Izzy's throat but she swallowed it back, determined not to be manipulated or charmed or fooled or anything she didn't choose to be. 'I am very, very angry with you,' she confided as she sank down in the chair he had yanked out for her. 'But I'm also very hungry, so we'll take a rain check on the shouting for now. Aren't you joining me?' Izzy prompted as he too sat down but there was no food at his place, only a cup of coffee.

'I have already eaten.' And it had not been an enjoyable meal with his uncle, the Regent, Rafiq reflected, his mind sliding back to that uncomfortable experience.

'Twins!' Jalil had pronounced, rubbing his hands together with incredulous glee. 'This is a very special young woman you have brought to us.'

Rafiq had dug deep to extract his innate honesty and had said what he knew would cause distress. 'This is a young decent woman, with whom I spent one night...'

His uncle surveyed him with tolerance. 'But Allah saw more clearly and saved you,' he breathed with genuine emotion, glossing over his nephew's sinful encounter. 'This woman is *meant* to be your wife.'

A little less naïve, Rafiq nodded, accepting that necessity. He was a crown prince and he wasn't stupid. He knew that the next generation was as important to the stability and popularity of the monarchy as he was. All those years wed to Fadith he had known he was a failure in providing that necessity, in fulfilling that occasionally despairing need a woman could have when it came to conceiving a child. He still could not *quite* accept that he could have unborn children on the way because, on his terms, it *was* a miracle…with difficulty, he dragged himself back into the present.

Izzy spared Rafiq a single glance but his lean, darkly handsome features stayed stamped on her brain like the ultimate blueprint of perfection. Her hands a little unsteady, she picked up her knife and fork.

'So tell me about the fiancée,' she invited, sweetly sarcastic.

'There isn't one. I'm *not* engaged. I did not contradict your misapprehension in Oxford because I was not in a position to explain that I had, however, recently agreed to remarry and why. As future King I am expected to take a wife. But no particular woman has yet been put forward for the role.'

While relieved that no other woman was involved in their plight to be hurt by her pregnancy, Izzy still made a stabbing motion with her knife in his direction. 'You didn't tell me who you were! You left me with no way of contacting you,' she condemned thinly. 'I had to go and talk to the receptionist at the rental agency to discover your identity. Why weren't you honest?'

In a powerful surge of energy, Rafiq rose from his chair and strode across the room, wheeling round before swinging back to face her again. Already, he was fighting the sensation of feeling trapped. 'Honesty would've changed everything between us. Pretending that I was an ordinary businessman kept it relaxed.'

Unimpressed, Izzy lifted her chin. 'The truth is always preferable,' she told him.

'I also liked the fact that you treated me as an equal and that you would have no reason to go and report your night with a prince to the tabloid newspapers who deal in such sleaze.'

'I didn't get a night. I got an hour in bed,' Izzy breathed tightly, wondering if he had been subjected to tabloid exposure of that nature at some stage, resolving right there and then to look it up and devour every word of sleazy revelation. She lifted cool hands to her hot cheeks, wondering what was wrong with her brain, why she would even *think* of doing such a crazy thing.

'And it was a wonderful hour,' Rafiq sliced back at her provocatively, his resolve to be calming taxed by her prickliness and the wall of distrust etched in her once clear eyes.

'It was an hour that destroyed all my future plans,' Izzy told him, furious that he was wriggling adeptly out of all her accusations. He had more lives than a cat, she decided resentfully. 'I love children but I wasn't planning to have any until I was much older. I wanted to finish my education and get my career started before I even thought of settling down. Now that I'm pregnant my ability to follow those plans has been seriously compromised.'

'I agree. Children will certainly limit your freedom, which is why I have every intention of ensuring that that accident of fate does not destroy your future,' Rafiq intoned silkily. 'This is not a development which either of us foresaw but we must make the best of it.'

'I doubt that a royal prince knows very much about making the best of anything!' Izzy parried angrily.

'I didn't *choose* this life, Izzy,' Rafiq fielded almost harshly. 'I was born into it and it imposed frustrating limits even when I was a little boy. Couldn't do this, couldn't do that, couldn't be seen to do many things as future King, couldn't be allowed to do anything that might seem too bold or different or aggressive or dangerous. There was an endless list of prohibitions and rules to follow, so, yes, I *do* know a great deal about making the best of a situation.'

Disconcerted by that flood of blunt explanation, Izzy lost colour and dropped her head. 'I'm in a snippy mood…but look on the bright side, at least I'm not shouting.'

Rafiq moved closer, his extraordinary eyes a mesmeric pure gold fringed by well-defined inky lashes. 'Must we dispute? Cannot we…even for one short minute…*celebrate* the conception of our children?'

'C-celebrate?' Izzy stammered and stared back at him in stark disbelief.

'Yes, celebrate,' Rafiq countered forcefully, leaning back against the footboard of the bed. 'You said that the truth is always preferable and I will not lie to you. That you have conceived feels like a miracle to me. It is amazing news and I am overjoyed…'

'Overjoyed,' Izzy almost whispered in her astonishment.

'I thought I couldn't have children,' he reminded her drily. 'And because of that inability, my younger brother was going to be forced to marry young to provide me with an heir to the throne.'

Izzy frowned. 'Why can't *he* be your heir?'

'It doesn't work that way in Zenara's constitution. Zayn's child being accepted as an heir would have been a big enough change to the usual direct line of succession from the eldest son. That I have conceived my own child makes life simpler for everyone,' he completed.

Her heart had been warmed by the notion of

her conception being worthy of celebration. Such an attitude radically changed everything because it was far removed from her far more prosaic expectations, which had run the gamut from Rafiq utterly denying that he could be the father to his having her conveyed back to the airport with a suitcase of cash to keep her quiet.

'Aren't you even about to ask me how it happened when I told you that I was on the pill?' Izzy prompted.

Rafiq shrugged. 'Does one question a miracle? I believe in fate.'

'Apparently a course of antibiotics can stop birth control working properly, so that may be what contributed to the…er…miracle,' she extended awkwardly. 'And the episode with the condom, of course.'

'Twins,' Rafiq pronounced with a slashing smile, ignoring that reminder. 'Could be boys, could be girls, could be one of each. That's even more exciting.'

'I'm surprised but delighted that you're pleased about the development. However, it doesn't sort out the problems,' Izzy remarked stiffly.

'There won't be any problems to worry about once we're married,' Rafiq countered with supreme assurance. 'Any problems you foresee will vanish.'

'And I'd vanish too if that were the *only* solution,' Izzy declared dizzily, stunned at that response, that apparent assumption that marriage was the only possible answer to their dilemma. 'I'm only twenty-one. I don't want to get married to anyone. I haven't even started living my life yet. For goodness' sake, I only had sex for the first time a couple of months ago!'

Rafiq registered that he had a problem and one he had not foreseen. For too long he had been encouraged to view himself as a matrimonial prize in terms of rank and wealth, his apparent infertility his only flaw. But the immediacy of Izzy's rejection showed him that rank and wealth meant nothing to some women. It was a supreme irony, he conceded grimly, that even though he didn't want to marry any woman her lack of greed and ambition might also have raised a tiny spark of enthusiasm in him for the venture.

'We will discuss it tomorrow,' he breathed in a driven undertone, emotions he didn't want pulling at him, refusing to allow him to embrace his usual cool-headed thought processes. He had learned to be unemotional during his first marriage, had learned that it was the only safe way to cope with doing his duty. He could not change that mindset, not when once again he had no other choice but to surrender his freedom. Lightning *could* strike twice in the same life, he acknowledged, but at least this time he had the joy of becoming a father to lighten the load…

CHAPTER FIVE

A COUPLE OF hours after Rafiq left Izzy alone, she slid into the big bed with a sigh of appreciation for its comfort.

She couldn't believe that she was tired again after napping throughout most of the afternoon but that had been one of the warnings given by the doctors. A multiple pregnancy would take more out of her than a singleton one and she would need more rest and a very healthy diet. She smiled, fingers creeping across her stomach as she thought about her babies.

It was an escape to think of them rather than the bombshell that Rafiq had dropped on her! Marriage? That didn't fit in with her plans or expectations at all. Rafiq was out of touch. Women didn't have to get married simply because they were pregnant these days, she soothed herself. Although being forced to take Rafiq to bed for the rest of her life could be an encouragement, she conceded guiltily, shocked and then amused by her drowsy reverie.

But then the bedroom door opened again and Rafiq strolled in, dark golden eyes widening a little when he saw her still awake, sapphire eyes rounding above the sheet with surprise, her hair tumbled across the pillow like a copper question mark.

'It's after midnight,' Izzy pointed out a little unsteadily. 'What are you doing here?'

'This is my bedroom.' Rafiq dropped the news without apology because he had a campaign to mount. Like it or not, freely choose it or not, he had to *make* Izzy marry him and he would do whatever he had to do to achieve that end result.

Izzy was so taken aback, she sat up against the pillows in a sudden movement. '*Your* bedroom? Why was I put in your room?' she gasped.

'Because everyone thinks we're married.'

'But we're *not!*' she protested vehemently.

'We know that,' Rafiq conceded. 'But to make a major announcement of the truth that you are pregnant and we are *not* married would kick off a huge scandal and I'm not prepared to do that.'

'Oh...' Izzy kind of saw his point, which only infuriated her. Unfortunately, it was *her* fault that everyone knew that she was pregnant.

'I owe Prince Jalil, my uncle and the Regent, more than that scandal after the hard work he has done to ensure that the Zenarian royal family is viewed with affection and respect again.'

'Again?' Izzy queried and then she shifted a hand, dismissing that mystery to concentrate on the here and now, which seemed rather more important. 'Couldn't you use another bedroom with the excuse that I'm pregnant and you don't want to disturb me?'

'No. Although it has been assumed that we were married in the UK, everyone also knows that we must have been apart for many weeks and to sleep anywhere but *with* you would look strange.'

Izzy breathed in very deep and compressed her lush pink lips. 'Then it looks like we're stuck with this sharing but it's not as though I'm planning to stay long, so I'm sure we can cope until I leave again. Then you can say we're divorced, can't you?'

Rafiq said nothing at all because there *was* nothing to say to that unwelcome suggestion. If it hadn't been for the twins she was expecting, they could have taken that road, but then they wouldn't have been in the situation in the first place had it not been for her pregnancy. His brain, which until that moment had been very much preoccupied with the prospect of becoming a father, took a sudden jolting hike in another direction as Izzy stopped hugging the sheet as though he were a potential rapist and let it fall to her lap. She was sporting something made of thin white cotton, the material so fine it outlined the ripe curves of her unbound breasts and displayed the darker circles of her pouting nipples. Rafiq went instantly hard as a rock and turned away lest she notice the desire his neatly tailored trousers could not conceal.

Izzy shifted over to what she had chosen as her side of the bed and told herself that she was *not* going to watch Rafiq undress. But she did, while for the entire space of each nail-biting second assuring herself that she would naturally close her eyes and stop peeking, *perving* on him like some sort of sex-starved woman.

After all, she was no longer that naïve any more, she told herself briskly. Unhappily, for some inexplicable reason, having seen Rafiq naked before didn't seem to be enough to satisfy her renewed curiosity or her fresh interest. The shirt dropped to the floor and her gaze hungrily roamed over his muscular brown torso as if she had never seen a man's chest in her life. A sort of invasive heat source entered her pelvis at the same moment as she appreciated the corrugated musculature lining his eight-pack, not to mention that Adonis belt of a vee that magically appeared as he began removing the suit trousers. Her nipples peaked and her body shifted restively below the sheet as she noted the dark arrow of hair disappearing below the waistband of his boxers and the sizeable bulge still covered there. And that was the point where shame made her shut her eyes tight, castigating herself for her inability to do so earlier.

Was it her fault that he was so absolutely magnificent naked that she wanted to put her hands all over him? Explore, touch, trace, *tease*? She buried her burning face in a pillow, praying for her composure to return before he registered how ill at ease she was simply sharing a bed with him again. After all, been there, done that, got more than a T-shirt out of it, why should sleeping with him in the same bed seem so much more dangerously intimate?

Rafiq went for a shower, a freezing-cold one, keen to dispel the treacherous pulse of arousal in case his condition gave her the impression that he wanted more. *Of course*, he wanted more of the best sex he had ever had, he scoffed at himself, but he wouldn't do anything about it or make any kind of approach. He might have taken advantage of her once, but he wasn't about to repeat that mistake. The mother of his unborn children deserved better than that; she deserved his respect, his consideration. And the streak of dark, highly sexed wildness in him that he always kept chained up and suppressed would not get a single chance to escape, he swore inwardly.

Taut with discomfiture from her most recent reflections, Izzy waited until she felt his weight depress the mattress before stretching out a hand to switch off the light. She couldn't expect him to sleep with the light on all night as she had planned to do because she didn't like waking up anywhere strange when she was half-asleep. She wasn't a kid any more. She could sleep fine in the dark in an unfamiliar place, she told herself irritably.

Even so, it seemed to be taking her a very long time to fall asleep because she was so very aware of his presence in the bed. The bed was wide, long, the perfect fit for a wide-shouldered, long-legged male, but he put out heat like a furnace and she swore she could feel that unwelcome heat warming her back and it made her all twitchy and uneasy, a tightening deep inside her nagging at her nerves.

'Go to sleep, Izzy,' a voice murmured in the merciful darkness. 'I'm not about to jump you.'

In silence, her teeth gritted and she wouldn't let herself screech something back. He thought she was afraid of him now, did he? How dared he?

She wasn't a scared little kid! She compressed her lips and, cursing him thoroughly, lay as still as a corpse and eventually that did the trick and she drifted off to sleep.

Feeling too warm woke her up again. Moonlight was casting a little clarity into the room and she could see that it was still dark but that was the least of her problems, she registered, because she was welded up against a very masculine body like a second skin and, yes, he was too hot but, on another level, he felt *incredible*. Yet again her teeth clenched together even as a tiny little quiver thrummed through her. It was a case of mind over matter. It was perfectly normal to be attracted to him but, in the circumstances, it would be totally wrong to do anything about it. So, even though she wanted to flip over and investigate that warm hair-roughened, sun-darkened skin with all the wanton attention of a complete pervert, she wasn't about to do it, was she?

Even if she wasn't the *only* one of them with that kind of idea and physical urges at play? After all, she wasn't stupid. His arousal was aggressively firm against her hip. In fact, she felt rather smug about the truth that he wasn't impervious to her either. Why should she be the only one suffering?

'If you don't stop twitching and shifting, I'll…' Rafiq ground out in frustration.

'You'll what?' Izzy positively snarled as she flipped up into sitting position. 'Go on! Threaten me with some ghastly medieval punishment for breathing!'

'I was not about to threaten you but you're certainly not making this easy!' Rafiq snapped back thickly.

'Oh, excuse me,' Izzy said snarkily, flipping back the sheet to slide off the bed, the nightie flipping up to reveal the stretch of shapely legs for his bemused appraisal. 'You're the one who had an arm round me!'

'I thought that if I held you, you might stop moving around so much and keeping me awake!' Rafiq grated. 'I'm sorry. I'm not used to sharing a bed with anyone.'

'You were married for ten years,' Izzy threw back at him. 'How is that possible?'

'We didn't share a room,' Rafiq ground out.

Disconcerted by that admission, Izzy swivelled back to the sofa by the wall that she had been considering for what remained of the night hours. With a sigh, she curled up on it and closed her eyes. 'What sort of a marriage was it in which you didn't even share a room?' she prompted with helpless curiosity.

'I will not discuss that.'

Rafiq swore in his own language and sprang out of bed. Izzy opened her eyes again on over six feet of angry naked masculinity stooping over her and snatching her up off the sofa to settle her firmly back down on the bed. 'You are not sleeping any place else but *this* bed!' he thundered down at her.

'Rafiq…the domestic tyrant,' Izzy murmured softly. 'It's kind of sexy.'

Seriously perturbed by that unexpected comeback, Rafiq froze, for that was one word he would never have applied to himself. He shook off the label again. It was a superficial, silly comment, not intended to mean anything, certainly not any kind of invitation when she was so angry with him. 'We'll talk over breakfast,' he breathed in a driven undertone.

He would lay the facts out for her then. After all, the woman he remembered had been reasonable and rational. Presumably she retained those traits, even if she wasn't displaying them at the moment. Of course, he reminded himself ruefully, just like him she was struggling to deal with a situation she had not foreseen and the sudden destruction of her immediate plans for the future. If he made it clear that she could still walk away and *have* that future, he would be offering her a practical solution.

Izzy wakened and, finding herself alone in the bed, wasted no time in taking advantage of the privacy. Showering and washing her hair, she chose capri pants and a tee to wear, her small case and even smaller wardrobe for a hot climate not offering much of a choice. Her brain felt clear again and her anxiety level soothed, leaving her feeling equipped to deal with whatever Rafiq had to throw at her over breakfast.

The quiet little maid was waiting in the bedroom to escort her out into a long stone corridor and through a doorway into very bright light. The heat engulfed her like a blanket, disconcerting her after the air-conditioned cool of the interior of the building. She was ushered down a flight of steps and into the merciful shade of palm trees to find herself standing in a very pretty courtyard, crammed with lush tropical plants.

'I didn't realise how hot it would be,' she muttered, suddenly plunged back into awkwardness as Rafiq, immaculate in yet another designer-cut suit, sprang up from the table set beneath the trees. 'I haven't been abroad very often. Well, we only ever had one foreign holiday,' she told him reluctantly, not wanting to sound like a deprived child because she loved her parents very much and did not want to sound in any way critical of them.

No way was she about to tell Rafiq, with the kind of wealth she assumed he had, that money had *always* been a problem in her family and that the single holiday to more exotic climes she had enjoyed only a couple of years earlier had occurred when one of her father's business ventures unexpectedly did well. Of course, the doing well hadn't lasted—it never did—and the business had eventually gone down in a torrent of debt, plunging them back into the normality of being a family for whom a holiday was a dream luxury.

'Where did the holiday take you?' Rafiq murmured easily, accustomed to setting people at ease in his presence, watching her settle nervously into the chair tugged out by one of the servants hovering.

'Spain. Matt was able to get down in the sand and act like a little boy for a change,' she recalled fondly of her little brother, whose need for a wheelchair prevented him from enjoying many of the pursuits available to an able-bodied child.

'You are close to your family,' Rafiq gathered, having watched her expressive face light up. 'I am very fond of my brother. I will introduce you to him soon. He is at school right now.'

'School's not something I miss,' Izzy muttered in what she knew had to sound like a gabbling rush but, really, continuing to look across the table at a guy who took your every single breath away at one glance was challenging. 'Maya was horribly bullied because she was so beautiful and clever. I was average.'

'I don't see you as average,' Rafiq cut in.

Izzy shrugged a tiny thin shoulder and ignored that pointed remark. 'You said we were going to talk. You don't need to work through this getting-to-know-you stuff to be polite with me.'

Rafiq breathed in deep and slow. 'Our children can only be recognised here if their parents are married. Obviously I want the children to have that option, to be able to take their place in Zenara as royals if they wish.'

Izzy had tensed and she sipped at her tea. 'But when you were talking yesterday, you didn't make it sound like being royal in Zenara was really that enjoyable,' she reminded him drily.

'I was raised in a totally different way from the way I will raise my own children. It was a different time in my country's history and a different set of circumstances. But neither of us can know what our children will want when they are grown up,' Rafiq reasoned. 'Don't you want them to have a free choice?'

Grudgingly, Izzy nodded because she hadn't thought through the royal connection. 'You're referring to titles, like you being a prince.'

'No, Izzy. I'm talking about much more. The firstborn of those twins will be my heir to the throne. I will be King when I reach my thirtieth birthday in eighteen months and my child will be the next in line, which is a very important role. If you don't marry me, both our children will be automatically excluded by law from an official role in Zenara. Yet they need to be living here to learn our language, our culture and to get to know their people.'

Izzy released her breath in a long sigh because she hadn't grasped just how deep that royal connection could go. Rafiq was going to be a *king*? Yes, she had already known that. So, how on earth had she contrived, even briefly, to forget such a fact? There she had been squabbling with him last night in bed as though he were just any ordinary Joe, when really he was anything but!

'In the light of that reality, I have a suggestion to make,' Rafiq murmured levelly.

Izzy looked up from the piece of fruit she was

slicing and let herself greedily focus on him, only for a few seconds, she bargained with her conscience. He had the same effect on her, she reckoned, as a major crush would have on a teenager. Only she had never experienced one of those crushes. During the teen years, she and her sibling had been far too busy handling family problems like bailiffs and debt collectors and keeping food on the table with part-time work as shop assistants. It was just there was something so ravishingly perfect about those lean dark, chiselled features and those eyes, *stunning*, gleaming with gold highlights, and then there were the lashes: inky, lush and curling. Her body heated to such an extent that she thought she might expire.

'A suggestion?' she said jerkily, dredging her attention off him again to concentrate on eating the fruit, which was much safer and more sensible, she told herself fiercely, exasperated by the manner in which her brain kept on wandering around him.

'That we marry now to legitimise our children and stay together until they are born,' Rafiq outlined with clarity. 'I need to be with you until the birth to support you, to be a *responsible* father.'

'You're a literal throwback to the Dark Ages,' Izzy muttered helplessly. 'But in an odd way, it's kind of sweet.'

'*Sweet?*' Rafiq growled.

'Most of the men I meet would run away from that level of responsibility,' she extended, reluctant to offend him. 'You're the opposite. Sorry, I interrupted you. You were suggesting that we stay together until after the birth…and then?'

'You and I go our separate ways,' Rafiq framed, releasing his breath. 'That agreement between us would leave all options open for all of us.'

Izzy nodded very slowly. Marry purely for the sake of that legal bond and then split up again? Yes, that did make sense to her. It *would* settle the essentials. It would give the twins their choices, whatever they might be, when they were adults and it would also leave both her and Rafiq free to continue with their lives. Even so, it certainly didn't feel like the answer to her every prayer and she didn't understand why it didn't.

'I think that would be almost perfect,' she told Rafiq, because her brain believed that and she squashed the sense of unease already threatening to rise inside her. 'After all, you can't be any keener on the idea of marrying a virtual stranger than I am.'

The strong lines of his fabulous bone structure went taut, showing off the intriguing hollows, and her heart jumped behind her breastbone. 'No…'

"One Minute" Survey

You get up to **FOUR books** <u>and</u> TWO Mystery Gifts...

> **ABSOLUTELY FREE!**

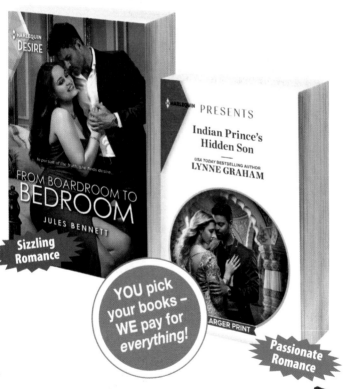

Sizzling Romance

YOU pick your books – WE pay for everything!

Passionate Romance

See inside for details.

Dear Reader,

Your opinions are important to us. So if you'll participate in our fast and free "One Minute" Survey, **YOU** can pick up to four wonderful books that **WE** pay for!

As a leading publisher of women's fiction, we'd love to hear from you. That's why we promise to reward you for completing our survey.

IMPORTANT: Please complete the survey and return it. We'll send your Free Books and Free Mystery Gifts right away. **And we pay for shipping and handling too!** *We pay for EVERYTHING!*

Try **Harlequin® Desire** books featuring the worlds of the American elite with juicy plot twists, delicious sensuality and intriguing scandal.

Try **Harlequin Presents® Larger-Print** books featuring the glamourous lives of royals and billionaires in a world of exotic locations, where passion knows no bounds.

Or TRY BOTH!

Thank you again for participating in our "One Minute" Survey. It really takes just a minute (or less) to complete the survey… and your free books and gifts will be well worth it!

Sincerely,

Pam Powers

Pam Powers
for Reader Service

"One Minute" Survey

GET YOUR FREE BOOKS AND FREE GIFTS!

✓ Complete this Survey ✓ Return this survey

1 Do you try to find time to read every day?
☐ YES ☐ NO

2 Do you prefer stories with happy endings?
☐ YES ☐ NO

3 Do you enjoy having books delivered to your home?
☐ YES ☐ NO

4 Do you find a Larger Print size easier on your eyes?
☐ YES ☐ NO

YES! I have completed the above "One Minute" Survey. Please send me my Free Books and Free Mystery Gifts (worth over $20 retail). I understand that I am under no obligation to buy anything, as explained on the back of this card.

☐ I prefer Harlequin® Desire 225/326 HDL GNWS

☐ I prefer Harlequin Presents® Larger Print 176 /376 HDL GNWS

☐ I prefer BOTH 225/326 & 176/376 HDL GNW4

FIRST NAME

LAST NAME

ADDRESS

APT.#

CITY

STATE/PROV.

ZIP/POSTAL CODE

he conceded almost guiltily half under his breath. 'I will always do my duty but my first marriage was not a happy one.'

Rafiq froze up even more as he felt those words slip from him because he had never once admitted to anyone what he had just admitted to her. Even so, the sky didn't fall, and no piercing shard of disloyalty pained him because he had long since adjusted to the absence of a woman who had, in truth, been as absent in life to him while alive as she was after she passed. 'I shouldn't have said that!' he breathed in a roughened undertone of discomfiture.

'Why not, if it's the truth?' Izzy murmured quietly, skating a soothing finger down over the clenched fist lying within her reach. 'All this will be easier if we try to be honest with each other.'

'Yes,' Rafiq conceded, censuring himself for that moment of weakness, that moment of un-guarded frankness that was very unlike him. Something about Izzy encouraged him to break free of his normal reserve and self-discipline. He would have to watch himself around her and not make a habit of such vulnerability.

Women disliked weak men and only weak men revealed emotion, he reflected grimly. He had learned that as a child when his mother pushed

him away and told him that boys didn't cry and
cling to their mothers. He had learned it as an adult
when he tried to reason with his childless wife and
referred to his own feelings and she went off into
hysterics, outraged that he could dare to mention
his side of their story and verbally abusing him
for that mistake.

'I will arrange the wedding.'

'Wedding?' she exclaimed in dismay.

'Not a normal one,' Rafiq qualified. 'A little
ceremony, which will only be witnessed by a couple of people in a quiet room here in this wing of
the palace.'

Izzy's frown evaporated. 'Because it has to be
secret,' she guessed. 'Well, that's lucky. I don't
have anything to wear for a proper occasion.'

'I will have appropriate attire brought to you.
My uncle will be one of the witnesses and a bride
in a dress of some kind will feel more normal to
him. He is a kind man, a good man but out of touch
with the modern world. Our situation has troubled
him deeply,' Rafiq confided again, compressing
his wide sensual lips on the suspicion that once
again he was saying too much, revealing too much.

Izzy nodded agreement and made herself
munch through a piece of toast very slowly because she was feeling a little queasy and hoping

that something a little more solid than fruit would settle it. Unhappily, the ruse didn't work and a few minutes later, she found herself plunging out of her seat like a madwoman and racing up the stairs and back to the bedroom again to find the bathroom.

She was genuinely horrified to glance up when she had finished being sick and discover Rafiq in the doorway. 'This is par for the course,' she pointed out defensively as she rinsed her mouth at the sink and reached for her toothbrush.

'The doctor will still visit. The palace has its own medical clinic. Now,' Rafiq breathed, suddenly at her elbow and bending down to scoop her up like a doll. 'You should rest until you feel a little better.'

He lowered her back down on the bed.

'But we will have to get some food into you that stays down,' he remarked worriedly. 'I will consult the doctor.'

And with that, Rafiq was gone, leaving her to dizzily study the space where he had been.

CHAPTER SIX

THEY WERE GOING to marry and, by the sound of it, quickly, Izzy reflected in a daze.

It wouldn't be a real marriage, of course, but it would enable her to build a proper foundation for her babies' futures and she wouldn't be fit to *be* a mother if she wasn't willing to make some sort of a sacrifice, would she? After all, her own mother had given up a life of comfort and ease to live on a shoestring for the sake of the twins she'd carried and to be with the man she loved.

Rafiq was clever too because he had stripped the facts down to the basics and left her without a leg to stand on with regards to the suggestion that they marry. She rolled her eyes at recognising how he had won the concession he wanted from her.

When the maid knocked and entered with another, explaining that they had brought an outfit for her to wear to meet the Regent, she was even more impressed by Rafiq's shrewd cover-up. Staging a secret wedding in a place stuffed with gossiping staff would have to be done with care but there could be no better excuse for her to get all dolled up than for the important occasion of meeting her husband's uncle, the Regent and current ruler of Zenara.

Evidently, there was a need for them to marry at speed before anyone could suspect that they were actually *not* married. She could only assume that any kind of scandal was viewed as a major catastrophe in the Zenarian royal family and suppressed a sigh. Her mother would have understood that viewpoint better than Izzy would have, considering that becoming an unwed mother-to-be had led to her mother being thrown out of her family. That same attitude, however, struck Izzy, the child of a different generation, as prehistoric.

Even so, if that was the way it had to be in Zenara she would play along for her babies' benefit, and in the bathroom she put on the long blue richly embroidered dress she had been brought. It was pretty but it looked like one of those national dress outfits people wore to dance in at country festivals and she smiled, returning to the bedroom to be draped in jewellery and have her hair fussed over. In the end she did her hair herself because her corkscrew curls had a mind of their own and putting them up in a more formal style took a familiar pair of hands. The jewels in the box opened for her perusal were utterly spectacular, she reflected, smoothing a reverential finger over the diamond and sapphire necklace at her collarbone, which was accompanied by matching earrings.

Rafiq strode into the bedroom and she froze because for the first time she was seeing him out of Western dress. He wore a long white tunic and cloak and a red-checked turban, the ends of which draped over his shoulder like a scarf. It was a mode of apparel that made him look very different, very...*very* fantasy sexy, she decided abstractedly, studying the clean sculpted lines of his devastatingly handsome features in awe. She stood up, her knees suddenly weak.

'You look amazing,' he told her.

Her eyes danced with amusement at his reaction to what felt like fancy dress to her but presumably seemed much more ordinary to him.

'Why are you laughing?' Rafiq demanded in bewilderment.

'Back home, only a micro miniskirt and a very revealing top would get me that reaction from a man,' she whispered.

Rafiq frowned. 'Do you dress like that when you go out?'

'No, never been a fan of putting it all out there,' she told him as he grasped her hand in his and led her down the corridor. The first thing she noticed was all the guards lining that corridor and then they were walking into a big sunlit room and a little portly man with a huge smile was coming towards her with an extended hand of welcome. The door closed behind them. Rafiq translated his uncle's warm greetings because the older man didn't speak much English, but it didn't matter because his smile and his twinkling dark eyes were wonderfully friendly and relaxed. Prince Jalil did not stand on ceremony.

A robed elderly man approached them and he spoke words to them both before directing them over to a table where Izzy and Rafiq were instructed to sign the marriage contract. Indeed, the wedding ceremony happened so fast and was completed so quickly that she almost asked Rafiq if that was really all there was to it. Happily, however, she was on her very best behaviour in such exalted company and engaged instead in replying to the Regent's polite questions about her family while Rafiq remained at her side, deftly translating.

'What now?' she murmured as Rafiq accompanied her back down the corridor.

'Now we escape the goldfish bowl of palace life,' Rafiq told her with resolve, guiding her downstairs and across an unbearably hot open space towards a helicopter.

'To go where?' she exclaimed. 'I haven't even packed!'

'You have nothing to pack. You brought hardly any clothes with you!' Rafiq pointed out. 'I have taken care of that problem.'

'Have you indeed? But—' Her voice broke off as he scooped her up in his arms to stow her in the helicopter and the rotor blades began spinning, making further conversation impossible.

Seated in the back of the helicopter, Izzy surveyed Rafiq in frustration. He hadn't told her where they were heading. He had implied that he had bought her clothes to wear. He had no right to do that, no right to make decisions without her input. They might be married but she was still struggling to accept the idea that bathroom guy, the father of the twins she carried, could now be her husband. And apparently, she had landed herself a bossy, I-know-best style of husband even if it was only for the next seven months or so...

She supposed he planned to visit their twins

when he was in London on business and that they would both be very polite and civilised following the divorce. After all, what else but a divorce could he be planning?

Thirty minutes later, she was peering out of the window beside her when she saw a huge building loom up ahead of them and she blinked in astonishment because initially she thought she was hallucinating. They had flown over endless miles of desert, only occasional rock formations and black tent encampments interrupting the emptiness, and then all of a sudden she saw the giant construction looming ahead. Cream and gold in colour, it had a great domed entrance and a forest of tall turreted walls. It resembled a fantasy cartoon castle yet the lines of it were modern, but it was still an utterly out-of-place property to find in what seemed to be the middle of nowhere.

'Where are we?' she questioned as the craft dropped down onto a helipad on a flat roof.

'Alihreza,' Rafiq informed her, his exotic bone structure taut, his intonation indicating some strong emotion but not one she could label. 'It has been mine since my father's death but I don't use it.'

'Then why now?' she prompted as he assisted

her from the craft to urge her through the blinding heat of exposure towards the building.

'Being here frees us from the goldfish bowl of palace life and gives us privacy. You can have your own room. I can go back to work and you can sun yourself by the pool and if we only meet once a day for dinner, nobody will even notice,' Rafiq completed with audible satisfaction.

Well, with her classic redhead's skin, quick to burn, she was unlikely to be sunning herself beside any pool, Izzy conceded, dazed by the piercing sense of hurt that assailed her in the wake of that little speech. He had brought them to this out-of-the-way spot so that he could reclaim his freedom and ignore her existence.

Why on earth *should* that make her feel hurt and rejected?

Hadn't they been honest with each other about their feelings? Rafiq was no keener on being married than she was, and it was natural that he would want to return to his normal way of life. He didn't want to be one half of a couple and feel forced to share a bed. He didn't want the annoyance of having to be seen to entertain a woman people believed was his wife.

It might hurt her pride, but she needed to come swiftly to terms with the reality that she was only a wife on a legal document and not in any other meaningful way.

Rafiq didn't owe her anything more and he wasn't pretending that he did either. That was honest, fair, she told herself firmly. They had had a one-night stand, not a relationship. A one-night stand and an accidental conception did not make a relationship.

An assembly of staff greeted them with a near reverential respect, which made her feel more of a fake than ever because she wasn't truly Crown Princess and future Queen—she was only a stand-in, a temporary aberration, Rafiq's contraceptive mishap…or miracle, depending on one's viewpoint, she adjusted ruefully.

A hail of polite introductions and smiles welcomed them to Alihreza before they were ushered into a lift that was as over-the-top opulent in mirrored design as the gilded marble corridors and staircases she had glimpsed.

'This place is spectacular,' Izzy murmured, staring in wonder at the tiers and arcaded terraces of carved stone walling that surrounded the huge central courtyard that sported a swimming pool, luxury seating areas and glorious vegetation.

'It is a monument to excess and corruption,'

Rafiq contradicted between compressed lips as he strode through grand double doors into a bedroom.

Thoroughly taken aback by that lofty judgemental statement, Izzy directed a bewildered glance at him.

Rafiq was poised by the window, his bronzed face in sunlight as he removed the ceremonial turban, running long brown fingers through his black luxuriant hair, that hair that *felt* like silk between her fingers. He was so beautiful at that moment that he made it hard for her to breathe, and something intimate tightened and clenched at her feminine core to send colour flying up into her cheeks.

Unnerved, Izzy made a show of examining her surroundings. It was a superb bedroom, awash with a jaw-dropping amount of luxury. In the simmering silence she ran a fingertip over the gilded trim on a nightstand and along the smooth crease of a delicate embroidered silk curtain.

'Your room is next door,' Rafiq informed her tautly, striding across the room to pull open the connecting door in invitation because the more he was exposed to her, the more he wanted her, which meant that keeping his distance made better sense. And he was *always* sensible, he reminded himself with resolve.

He couldn't have her, not now when their marriage was only supposed to be an empty charade, and it was a retrograde step to appreciate what he could not have. He saw that lush pink mouth and he craved it. She was like a fire in his blood, heating him up every time she came too close yet blissfully unaware of the effect she had on him. She had gazed back at him incredulously when he told her she looked amazing in that dress, utterly unable to see how the tight bodice cupped her full breasts and how the drape of the fabric outlined the curve of her generous hips, equally incapable of comprehending how a man who had already seen her naked could picture her shapely legs...*spread*.

Rafiq gritted his teeth at that crude thought and image, particularly at experiencing it in the place most notorious for his father's carnal transgressions. Maybe the blood in him *did* run true, only fortunately for him his clean-living uncle had contrived to have more of a sobering effect on his principles than his dysfunctional parents had. Such troubling concepts and suspicions and insecurities had haunted Rafiq since he had been a teenager. Every time he craved sex for the sake of it, every time he wondered what it would be like to be with a woman who wanted him outside those few short days when she had the greatest chance of conceiving...

As if that declaration about her separate room hadn't punched what remained of her breath back out of her lungs, Izzy pinned a bright smile to her face since it seemed to be what Rafiq expected and she didn't like to disappoint him. Or maybe she wanted to hang onto what remained of her pride, a more cynical inner voice suggested as she strolled over to the open doorway, and then what he had said only minutes before roused her curiosity afresh and she turned back to him and probed inquisitively, 'A monument to excess and corruption?'

Lean, devastatingly attractive features grim, Rafiq turned brooding dark eyes back to her, thinking that she just had to go *there*, where nobody else dared in his radius. 'My father built this palace and ploughed millions into it, so that he could have somewhere *very* private and luxurious to entertain.'

'Well, maybe he was extravagant but surely in an oil-rich country that's not a hanging offence,' Izzy remarked uncomfortably, beginning to wish by his grave demeanour that she had left the subject alone.

Rafiq studied her with shielded eyes and decided it was time to tell her what was already widely known in Zenara, where his father's name was never ever mentioned in polite company. 'He held drug-fuelled orgies here with porn stars and hookers.'

'Oh…' For a split second, Izzy was frozen to the floor by shock and then she blinked rapidly, and a startled strangled snort of laughter was wrenched from her, her hand flying up to her parted lips in sincere apology and dismay. 'S-sorry,' she stammered. 'I was just thinking that this is one place where you wouldn't want to say, *If only the walls could talk!*'

Rafiq surveyed her in utter disbelief.

'I'm sorry, I'm sorry, but you're standing there like a pillar of doom,' Izzy told him helplessly. 'All ashamed and disgusted and miserable at having to tell me that. Why are you still so sensitive about it? Your father's gone! It *is* the past you're talking about, not the present, and you're not responsible for your father's choices.'

'It is not that simple,' Rafiq argued fiercely. 'He disgraced the royal house. There is no depravity he did not explore, no extravagance he did not commit!'

'When did he die?' Izzy asked more gently.

'Sixteen years ago…' Rafiq admitted flatly.

'And you're still angry, but you shouldn't still be feeling that so personally,' Izzy countered with conviction. 'It happened and can't be changed but the sins your father committed weren't yours and you should make the decision to let go of it all. Make that decision for your own sake. It *is* that simple.'

Rafiq was shaken by that straightforward and practical approach to the sordid heritage that had haunted and humbled him throughout his life.

'I mean, *every* family has secrets,' Izzy commented more thoughtfully. 'Some secrets are embarrassing, some are hurtful, some may even cruise close to illegality but there's nothing you can do about that. If it's your family, you're stuck with them and that background, but you certainly shouldn't feel guilty about their mistakes, particularly not if you choose to lead a different life from theirs. I mean, you *do*, don't you?'

Even more surprisingly in response to that enquiry, Rafiq found himself breaking out into spontaneous laughter that she could even ask such a question of him. 'Definitely not into orgies and the like,' he confirmed with a flashing smile, relishing her indifference to what he had told her and the obvious fact that it didn't change her attitude to him. 'But some people *do* believe that such behaviour as my father's is the result of bad blood and that such a man's children may follow in his footsteps.'

'Only really, *really* out-of-touch, prejudiced people,' Izzy opined confidently.

'I am not oversensitive on the subject,' Rafiq felt the need to declare even though he knew he was glossing over the truth, indeed possibly outright lying. After all, his father's sins had been used like a stick to beat him with throughout his life, changing him, marking him, rebuking him, warning him of the danger of excess in any field. Having someone simply laugh inappropriately and remind him that his father's mistakes were not his to repent was a little like being suddenly busted out of a prison cell with bars that he hadn't even realised existed.

'Well, if this is my room, I'll leave you to it!' Izzy breezed, stepping through the doorway and beginning to close the connecting door.

'No!' In an abrupt movement, Rafiq crossed the room and dragged the door open again.

'No?' Izzy queried in surprise as she spun back. 'But I *thought*—'

'This far we have not had much of a wedding day,' Rafiq breathed in taut continuation. 'No celebration, nothing…'

Izzy shrugged a tiny dismissive shoulder, her head high, her chin at an I-can-cope-with-anything angle. 'We're not a real couple,' she pointed out quickly.

'We may as well be,' Rafiq countered, brilliant dark-as-Hades eyes locked to her triangular face, lingering on her pale flawless skin and the brightness of her bluer than blue eyes. 'Tonight, we will do something different…'

'Don't think there's a lot of *different* around this neck of the woods,' Izzy warned him ruefully, having only seen sand and more sand out of any of the windows that looked beyond the walls and the courtyard. And Izzy didn't *like* sand, had never liked sand, whether it was sand on a beach or sand in a sandpit when she was a kid. Sand in giant rolling dunes that formed the entire landscape left her cold.

'We will dine in the desert this evening,' Rafiq proposed, striving to think feminine, romantic, even frilly and getting absolutely nowhere in his imagination because he had absolutely no experience in that line. Instead he was forced to settle on an experience that he was pretty sure she could not previously have encountered.

'Oh…' Izzy was just quick enough to kill the grimace threatening her facial muscles. 'Well, that would be different, *special*,' she added hastily, not wanting to be picky or ungracious because there truly wasn't much available in the way of alternative options.

'The stars are amazing at night,' Rafiq told her with sudden warmth, his smile illuminating his bronzed features like the sun and dazzling her. 'The desert at night is wondrous.'

Engulfed by that astonishing smile, Izzy decided she could bear to picnic in a mud puddle should that be what was required of her.

Vanishing back into his own room, Rafiq stripped for a shower and wondered why he had suggested dinner in the desert. It was surely basic courtesy to ensure that his bride enjoyed her time in Zenara and for him to act as a considerate host? *Even though he had planned to avoid her?* his hind brain prompted. And beneath the beat of the shower, Rafiq groaned, comprehending his change of heart with a clarity that surprised him.

Izzy was *not* Fadith. In nature, she was not remotely similar to his first wife. She was a totally different woman. Just as the handful of women he had had sex with in recent years could also have been dissimilar, only he had never given them the chance to prove that, had never got to know them in any but the most superficial of ways. He had never spent the night with anyone until Izzy and

had never allowed an encounter to stretch into a
second night.

Izzy, however, was a unique case. *'We're not a
real couple,'* she had said, and while in one essential way that was true since they did not plan to
remain together, in other ways it was quite distinc-
tively untrue, Rafiq reasoned seriously. Of course,
his outlook on marriage was very different from
hers. Weddings were fun occasions in the West,
associated with romantic love and deeply optimistic hopes. But being born royal, Rafiq had never
expected that kind of marriage. He had always
known that he was unlikely to get to choose his
wife for himself and that he would have to simply make the best of whichever woman he married. That awareness had made him realistic and
practical.

What Izzy had yet to accept was that, even
without those Westernised notions of hers about
marriage, she was *still* his wife and was *still* the
mother of his unborn children, a bond that would
create an unbreakable lifelong tie between them.
And when she did reach that real-world state of
acceptance, how would she feel then? How could
he possibly know?

He was still marvelling that she was willing to
surrender custody of their offspring and leave her

children behind in Zenara while she returned to the UK to pursue her career plans. She was a lot younger than he was, he reminded himself, and still defiantly determined to reclaim the life she had expected to have, and he understood that tenacious streak of hers. Even so, she had seemed softer, more sentimental and had made it very clear that family meant a lot to her...

But then what did he know about a mother's emotions, most particularly a career-orientated modern mother? he asked himself cynically. Having birthed him, his own mother had not seemed to care whether he was alive or dead, having never shown any further interest in him. At a very young age he had realised that not all women were maternal. It wasn't *every* woman who wanted to raise her own child, take on that responsibility for another being's welfare and limit her own freedom accordingly. He had not the slightest doubt that, had it not been for the royal nursery staff, he would have starved and cried without comfort as a baby. He wasn't making a poor judgement of Izzy's character, he assured himself staunchly, just as he hadn't judged his mother for the same lack of interest. After all, he freely acknowledged that his father had been no more concerned than his mother about their son's well-being. And with his private jet at her disposal, Izzy would be able to come back and visit their children any time she wanted…

In the bedroom next door, Izzy cradled her mobile phone and tried to work out what she could afford to tell her sister when she called her. And she *had* to call Maya because they had never been out of contact for so long.

'Where the *heck* have you been?' her twin shrilled down the line with worried emphasis. 'I've been worried sick! You *vanished*… I mean, who can afford to do that on our income?'

Izzy registered that she had to come clean. 'I found out that I was pregnant,' she told her sister baldly.

'How the hell—' Maya exclaimed and then added with startling insight, 'Bathroom guy? I *knew* I wasn't getting the whole story.'

'Bathroom guy,' Izzy confirmed, grateful for once that her sibling was that quick on the uptake.

'Right, so you're *pregnant*,' her twin murmured with laden stress on that condition. 'And right now, I'm…er…working in Italy.'

'You got a job abroad?' Izzy gathered with admiration. 'Congratulations. I expect, considering how fast your talents have been snapped up, that the position pays very well?'

There was an unexpected silence before Maya responded brightly, 'The benefits are unbelievable. My stay in Italy promises to free Mum and Dad from *all* their financial problems!'

'My goodness,' Izzy muttered, undeniably impressed by her twin's superior earning power. 'But what a shame that the dream job has to be abroad!'

'Well, can't have everything,' her twin sighed feelingly. 'So, where are you?'

'Zenara,' Izzy admitted.

'Where's that?' Maya questioned, delighting Izzy with her ignorance. 'And you're living there with this guy?'

'Yes.' Izzy grimaced, reluctant to tell fibs to her sister and hoping she wouldn't ask too many more difficult questions. She would tell Maya the whole story when she got home again but if she spoke up now, her twin would be worried sick, and she didn't need that stress when she had just embarked on a demanding highly paid job in a foreign country. But sooner than that she would definitely have to tell Maya about Rafiq's true identity and share the news that they were married.

'He wants us to stay together until the babies are born,' she admitted.

'Babies…like *more* than one baby?' Maya exclaimed in excitement.

'Twins,' Izzy confirmed. 'But it's too soon to know the gender yet.'

'Heavens, I'm going to be an auntie!' Maya cried with satisfaction and the dialogue veered off awkward questions into territory that Izzy could more easily cope with.

'All right, you're being suspiciously silent here about the important stuff. Tell me all about bathroom guy.'

'He's…he's gorgeous.'

'You're not that shallow,' Maya told her.

Izzy reddened at her end of the phone. 'He's very responsible, decent, maybe a little old-fashioned.'

'Nothing to complain about there when you fall accidentally pregnant,' her twin commented bluntly. 'Why shouldn't he be responsible? They're his kids too. At least he's not trying to run away.'

'Rafiq is not the running-away type.'

Having completed her call, Izzy walked into the ridiculously large and luxurious dressing room off the bedroom and opened doors and drawers, amazed to find them packed with brand-new garments and she leafed through them in awe. Rafiq had *said* she had no clothes because she had only brought along a couple of casual summery outfits in her carry-on case and he had made good on that deficit, *so* good indeed that she was staggered by

his generosity. There were drawers full of fine lingerie, rails lined with dresses, both long and short,
and all appeared to be maternity wear. It was good
that he was aware of that issue with clothing, she
told herself even while her instincts shrieked no,
no, *no*, don't want that aspect to be so important
that it shadows everything else for him.

*So, you go and say thank you like a well-
brought-up woman,* she reflected, reasoning with
her less grateful self, crushing it down because she
was being *unreasonable*. After all, he wouldn't
have needed to marry her or clothe her had she not
been pregnant, therefore it was downright irratio-
nal to be annoyed that he was quite *that* aware of
her condition. And it was not as though she could
afford to buy a hot-climate wardrobe for herself or
any maternity wear, she reminded herself. In any
case her cropped jeans were already straining at
her thickening waist and all her bras were too tight.

Knocking on the door politely, she walked into
his empty bedroom.

'Rafiq!' she called lamely, knowing in frustration that there was no way she could track him
down easily in the giant building and simply hoping against hope that he was still somewhere
within hearing distance.

The bathroom door opened and he emerged, wrapped in a towel, and she grinned.

'So, back where we started, with you half naked,' she commented cheerfully, rejoicing in the vision of him standing before her, all lithe and bronzed and damp. 'I like it.'

Rafiq was shocked by that earthy honesty and struggled to hide it. Odd as it seemed, it had never really occurred to him that a woman might like to look at a man naked as much as a man liked to look at a woman and, acknowledging that, he felt off-puttingly out of his depth even though he was incredibly flattered and aroused by the appreciation that glowed in her sapphire eyes. That unabashed glow in her gaze had an immediate effect on him and he gritted his even white teeth, striving to suppress his arousal.

'I wanted to say thank you for the clothes…but there are so many,' she exclaimed. 'I'm never going to get to wear all of them!'

'You will be here for months,' Rafiq pointed out levelly. 'Through the hottest season.'

Izzy tried and failed to swallow as she studied him, her attention involuntarily glued to that tall, lean, powerful physique of his, the muscles indented in his torso that shifted with his every slight movement, the flatness of his stomach and the little dark silky furrow of hair there that snaked down out of sight below the towel. Her mouth ran dry. 'Not as hot as you,' she mumbled while thinking, I didn't just say that, *I didn't*.

'You find me…hot?' Rafiq breathed without any thought at all.

Colour claiming her cheeks in a feverish surge, Izzy simply nodded with a jerk.

The silence seethed, dark golden eyes welded to blue like heat-seeking missiles, and she felt her whole body leap into awareness, jolting her with embarrassing sensation as her breasts swelled and the peaks tightened and that hollow hungry pulse throbbed between the slender thighs she pressed tightly together.

A phone rang, breaking in like a sudden bucket of ice water flung over her heated skin, and she turned away in haste as he reached with a stifled apology for the mobile phone lying at the foot of the bed. She was crossing back into her own room again when he murmured abruptly, 'It's cold in the desert in the evening. Wrap up warm,' he advised.

Cold *and* sandy, she thought dolefully. Oh, joy.

CHAPTER SEVEN

THE NIGHT SKY was a great arching black velvet expanse spangled with white glittering stars and it was, indisputably, very beautiful. The fire crackled and burned with blue and orange flames that were almost hypnotic, light leaping and casting shadows over the robed and armed men guarding the encampment. Dinner in the desert with a crown prince demanded a substantial number of people in support and protection roles, Izzy reflected ruefully.

There was the cook and his helpers, who had slaved over a brazier to provide a wholly impractical elaborate meal that ran to several courses. There were also Rafiq's bodyguards, the maid hovering for Izzy's benefit, lest she might need some service carried out. There was a black cloth tent behind them for their comfort and given the excuse she would have retreated to it because it

looked cosy and she *was* horribly cold, in spite
of the layers she wore. Across the fire, musicians
pounded skin drums softly, another man plucking
at a stringed instrument that resembled a mando-
lin while two more wielded flutes. The music was
rhythmic and melodic, the muted beat of the drums
humming through her bones.

'My brother will visit us tomorrow. He is eager
to meet you,' Rafiq told her quietly, after they had
eaten.

With their backstory, Izzy winced a little at the
prospect. 'What have you told him about us?'

'Very little. He has no interest in the details.
Let me be blunt—you are the answer to Zayn's
every prayer,' Rafiq declared with amusement.
'With me married and on track to have an heir,
he finally has the freedom to do as he likes. He
will join the army, train at Sandhurst, abseil down
cliffs, shoot and blow up things. The active life of
a professional soldier has always been his dream,
but it was deemed too dangerous for the younger
son who still had to marry and produce an heir
and he was barred from it until now.'

'It's good to know that our…er…misfortune
will bring someone else a happy result.'

'Our children are *not* a misfortune,' Rafiq sliced
in with ruthless bite, grasping her slender fingers

in emphasis, and then his ebony brows shot up and knotted into a frown. 'Your skin is like ice…why didn't you tell me that you were so cold?' he demanded, vaulting upright and carrying her up with him in the sudden movement. 'We'll use the tent.'

He urged her inside and she blinked rapidly, momentarily blinded by the brilliance of the many intricate jewelled glass lanterns that hung from the poles above them and sprinkled the soft rugs on the floor with slanting shards of rainbow colour. He tugged her down onto an opulent sofa scattered with cushions and rubbed her slender spine as if he could somehow force heat into her chilled bones.

Taking in her luxury surroundings, she laughed. 'Your people can't really have carted around all this furniture when they travelled into the desert.'

'Of course not, but this is what my father taught the staff at Alihreza to do. He never set foot out in the desert without insisting on every possible comfort,' Rafiq told her wryly, arranging a velvet throw round her shoulders and then laughing as he looked down at her, touching the pink tip of her small nose. 'You're bundled up in so much cloth you look like a baby being swaddled!'

Izzy gazed up into stunning dark golden eyes fringed with black curling lashes and her heart skipped an entire beat, her body engulfed by such a wash of heat that she broke out in nervous perspiration and quickly shrugged her shoulders to emerge from the cocoon of cloth she was wrapped in. 'Just being in here warms me up,' she muttered awkwardly, ducking her head down to break that visual connection in case he guessed what being that close to him did to her wretched hormones.

Long brown fingers pushed up her chin and their eyes met again, colour warming her cheeks, her lips softly parting. A growl broke free low in his throat as he scanned that pink pouting invitation and his mouth crashed down on hers with a raw hunger that stole her breath away.

'I'm burning up for you,' he breathed raggedly as he finally wrenched his mouth from hers to allow her to catch her breath.

Staring at him, Izzy sucked in oxygen like a drowning swimmer until instinct drove her back for more of his mouth, hunger sizzling through her like a forest fire that had only required a spark to blaze. Her hands slid up over his shoulders and locked in the lush depths of his hair, a gasp sounding from her as his tongue tangled with hers and then plunged deep, sending a piercing shard of need arrowing to the very heart of her.

Without warning, she was on her back on the sofa and Rafiq was engaged in impatiently extracting her from her clothes and removing his own. Nothing had ever felt so desperate for her as that overpowering need to feel *his* skin against *her* skin.

'We weren't going to do this,' Rafiq growled the reminder as he straddled her in the act of pulling off his T-shirt before jerking down the zip on his jeans.

'Shut up,' Izzy said resolutely, running exploring hands appreciatively up over his bare bronzed torso and rejoicing in the sheer heat and masculinity of him.

Rafiq came down to her again like a man compelled by an unseen force, seeking her parted lips again, fiercely exploring and plundering. Izzy moaned low in the back of her throat as his wide chest crushed her throbbing nipples and his pelvis sank into contact with hers but she still had way too many clothes on and her hips bucked upward as she fought to shimmy out of her tailored wool trousers. Rafiq rolled off her onto the floor with a stifled groan. 'This is crazy!' he ground out in frustration.

Izzy rolled upright and shimmied with shameless haste out of her trousers. 'Only if you overthink it.'

'I always overthink stuff,' Rafiq admitted hoarsely.

Izzy had the cure for him, she decided as she sank down on her knees in front of him and tugged at the waistband of his jeans. The boxers went down with them, exposing the thick length of him. She licked her lips and just went for the challenge, hoping enthusiasm was more important than experience and from his first husky sound of pleasure she was lost in a sensual daze.

'I want to come inside you,' Rafiq husked, his deep voice soft and hoarse as he pulled her back up to face him again.

Unexpectedly, he then dropped down on his knees to peel her panties out of his path and nuzzle against the tender flesh between her slender thighs. All control was torn from her as he explored the swollen dampness at her core where she was so unbearably sensitive.

Izzy quivered with excitement and shook until he lifted her, hands cupping her hips and, in a feat of strength that took her breath away, brought her down on him with an urgent hiss, his body meeting hers and thrusting home with an efficiency that sent her heart racing like a bullet. He went down on the floor and hooked her legs over his shoulders and began to move with awesome speed and ferocity, grinding down into her receptive body with all the urgent demand and force she craved.

As frantic as he was in that driving need for completion, she writhed under him in a frenzy, rising up to welcome every thrust.

The pressure tightening within her was an uncontrollable force of nature that dominated everything. When he sent her soaring and, with a harsh gasp of completion, buried his face in her tumbled hair, she felt as though she blacked out at the apex of her climax because it was so blinding, so utterly intense. Shaken by that raw physical intensity, she trembled as spasms of delight continued to ripple through her in pulsating waves.

Rafiq lifted himself off her in a fluid movement and then hunkered down to lift her up into his arms.

He stalked into the bathing facilities tacked onto the back of the tent and pressed the shower lever. Water streamed down her overheated body, plunging her from one temperature into coolness. She shivered and used the shower gel to freshen herself up as quickly as she could. As she emerged, Rafiq engulfed her in a giant towel and dried her off.

'I was rough. Did I hurt you?' Rafiq murmured, those glorious eyes locked to her and visibly anxious.

'No, I *love* your passion,' she confided in an involuntary rush, still stunned by the entire experience they had shared.

'And I yours,' Rafiq murmured thickly, scooping her damp naked body into his arms and holding her close. 'But I didn't intend this to happen.'

'Shush…' Izzy urged, resting a finger against his wide sensual mouth.

'I thought we could manage our relationship most effectively by becoming friends.'

Izzy rolled her eyes as he tugged a throw over her to keep her warm. 'We're never going to be friends. I'm too attracted to you,' she told him baldly, shaken by her own boldness but preferring to be honest. 'I know that's a complication we don't need but, since you seem to be feeling the same way, we might as well just go with the flow for the present.'

'I don't think I've ever gone with the flow with anything,' Rafiq admitted, black lashes lowering over his beautiful dark golden eyes as he studied her. 'How attracted is attracted?'

'Hungry for compliments…right?' Izzy grinned up at him, absolutely charmed by that need she saw in him then while she was in her relaxed state and able to be observant.

'It is a serious challenge for me to keep distance between us,' Rafiq confessed.

'Well, we just lost that battle,' Izzy pointed out without too much concern, relieved as she was to know that he was struggling with the concept of a platonic bond in the same way that she was. 'You're accustomed to rules and following them. But you can't make decisions on my behalf. I couldn't do friends with you right now…maybe some time in the future when we're a little more distant from recent events. Let's just keep it casual.'

Rafiq released his breath on a slow measured hiss. In relationships, he preferred a pre-set agenda with every aspect carefully considered in advance. That approach left little room for misunderstandings or sudden emotional squalls. In comparison, he had never extended casual to more than one night with a woman and to be married and involved in a casual sexual relationship with his wife struck him as all kinds of wrong and dangerous, indeed much more likely to cause confusion and toxic feelings when they finally separated. And yet he still wanted her, he *wanted* Izzy more than he had ever wanted anything, and the knowledge that she carried his children only turned him on even more and made it even harder to take a step back. He lounged back on the sofa, cradling her in his arms, and struggled to relax while his libido was stirring him again to renewed hunger for her.

'You're so tense,' Izzy sighed against his chest, revelling in the damp musky scent of his skin, one hand idly stroking a satin-smooth shoulder. 'Tell me about your parents. What's your last memory of them?'

Rafiq groaned at that unfortunate question, which nobody had ever asked him before, but he was in the mood to be honest, shedding the guilt that that recollection always imbued him with. 'I was hiding behind a pillar and listening to them having a violent argument about the fact that my mother was pregnant with Zayn. She wanted a divorce and an abortion. She didn't want another child.'

'Good grief…' Izzy whispered, lifting her head to look down at him, concern palpable in her troubled blue eyes. 'What age were you?'

'Ten or so.' Rafiq compressed his lips, feeling his tension drain away as he shared that memory. 'I was spying on them because my parents were virtually strangers to me. They spent almost all their time abroad and I was insanely curious about them.'

'Naturally you were. Does Zayn know about what you overheard?'

'Of course not. I would never have shared that scene or what was said then with him.'

'Why didn't they take you abroad with them?'

'A child wouldn't have fitted in with their life-styles. My father was an unrepentant drug addict and my mother loved to party. Neither of them had any desire to settle down and be parents. By that stage my mother was tired of my father's infideli-ties and she wanted out of the marriage, but if she divorced him without his agreement, she would have lost the unlimited spending power she en-joyed and in the end she couldn't face that pros-pect.'

'So, they stayed together,' Izzy gathered.

'And she died of pre-eclampsia when Zayn was born. My father was negligent in not ensuring that she had the very best medical care. But by then they were already living separate lives.'

'Why was he like that? *So* uncaring?'

'I don't know. His mother died young and his father was elderly, which meant that he was only twenty when he came to the throne, too immature to have such power and wealth. He neglected his duties to chase a jet-set lifestyle across Europe and quickly fell into drugs. He built Alihreza because he was getting pressure to spend more time in Ze-nara, and he could only face that if he could have a very private bolt-hole where he could continue to indulge in drugs and sex.'

'Did he die from an overdose?' Izzy whispered.

'No, someone poisoned him, which is why I have a food taster.'

'A *food* taster?' she gasped in disbelief. 'But those times *I* cooked for you…'

'I broke the rules set by the executive council for my upbringing,' Rafiq murmured with amusement glinting in his dark golden eyes. 'How could I have explained a food taster while I was posing as an ordinary businessman?'

'Why was he poisoned?' A shiver ran through Izzy. 'That's seriously scary.'

'He had made so many enemies. He was a notorious womaniser. He slept with just about every woman around him and it's unlikely that they were *all* willing partners. I've always believed that it was a revenge killing. His death was exhaustively investigated but nobody was ever brought to trial. Now may we please talk about something else? I have answered all your questions.'

Izzy had lots more to ask but she suppressed the words bubbling in her throat because she could see that trudging through that weighty back story of his had loaded him down with unhappy recollections. And she didn't blame him—she really didn't blame him. Although he had been born into almost unimaginable status and wealth, he had not

enjoyed the love, support and security that all children needed to thrive.

'So, both your parents were gone and that's why
your uncle had to raise you and your brother,' she
summed up quietly.

'And we could not have had a better guardian,'
Rafiq sighed. 'Becoming Regent and agreeing to
raise his nephews was a huge responsibility for
Jalil to take on and he has never been a man who
enjoyed the limelight, yet he did it because he felt
it was his duty.'

Gently settling her down on the sofa, he stood
up and began to get dressed. 'Let's return to the
palace,' he urged. 'It's getting late and you must
be tired.'

But Izzy wasn't tired. As she was shuttled back
along a rough track in a four-wheel drive, Izzy's
brain was teeming with thoughts. They had become intimate again. She hadn't planned that,
hadn't truly had time to consider that aspect of
their marriage because one minute they had been
two separate people and the next they had been
married. Keeping it casual wouldn't come naturally
to her, she acknowledged ruefully. But, somehow,
she had found herself saying what she believed that
Rafiq needed to *hear* to relax with her.

He had felt trapped in his first unhappy marriage. He hadn't said so, but she had guessed how he felt about those years, years spent with a woman she didn't believe he had loved. She definitely didn't want him to feel trapped with *her*. She wasn't going to attach strings just because sex with Rafiq was mind-blowing. She wasn't about to tell him that though, wasn't an idiot. What had started out as a random, utterly unexpected first-time sexual experience had turned into something more for her, but she wasn't about to share that either. Her feelings were getting deep and complicated where he was concerned. Feelings that made her feel attached and involved in a way she was terrified of being but somehow couldn't help, feelings that were stronger than common sense and self-preservation. But was that really so surprising when the man she had married was also the father of the twins she carried?

Right now, her hormones had to be firing on all cylinders because of the pregnancy, she reasoned anxiously, and that might well be why her emotions were all over the place. It was even possible that she could be imagining the sense of attachment pulling at her.

Closing a firm hand over hers, Rafiq urged her into his bedroom with him and closed the door.

'What am I doing in here?' she muttered. 'I thought you liked your privacy.'

'Not when you're around,' Rafiq said succinctly, staring down at her with hooded dark golden eyes alight with sexual heat, his well-defined jaw line taut and beginning to shadow with stubble, accentuating his beautiful mouth. He looked so hot, her knees wobbled, butterflies flying loose in her stomach. 'Give me one good reason why I'd want to sleep alone.'

'Thought you preferred it that way.'

'Thought the same about you,' Rafiq incised, lean brown fingers rising to frame her flushed face. 'Got that wrong, *very* wrong.'

Enthralled by the dark liquid sexiness of his deep voice, Izzy tilted her head back to have a better view of him and that was a mistake because her mouth ran dry when she met the scorching heat of his appraisal. Her body reacted instantly, nipples tightening, pelvis clenching, that hollow ache between her thighs stirring afresh.

'Five minutes after I have you, I want you again,' Rafiq husked.

Her hands lifted and settled at his narrow waist to steady herself and she shifted closer, feeling the heat of his lean, powerful physique soak through the barrier of their clothes. She shivered, the strength of the pull he exercised over her unnerving her as she tried to fight it. It was the work of an instant for him to haul her fully into his arms and detach her from the cloak she had been wrapped in, casting it aside to unbutton the tunic she wore beneath.

'Rafiq…' she began.

'Tell me you don't want me.'

Her breath snarled up in her throat because she couldn't lie to him, couldn't lie to herself, had never in her life before realised that hunger could be so overwhelming that she could barely think, never mind speak in the grip of it. 'Can't do that,' she muttered in a pained whisper.

He gathered her up into his arms and brought her down on the big bed. 'A little taste of you only makes me want more. It makes me greedy.'

As his lips closed around a straining pink nipple, her spine arched, and she gasped helplessly in response. Shimmering dark golden eyes surrounded by dense black lashes gripped hers and her heartbeat hammered, liquid heat shooting straight to her core. He spread her over the bed and worked a skilled path down over her squirming body, teasing at the more receptive spots, lingering at his leisure when her response was more immediate, toying with her as her movements grew more agitated. It was a slow burning torment after the swift release he had granted her earlier when his dominant masculinity had been exactly what she craved.

Her control was hanging by a thread, tiny tremors rippling through her as she stayed poised on the edge of climax, frantically seeking that ultimate goal. He swiped his tongue across her exquisitely sensitive bud and her whole body rose in a whoosh of sensation, fierce arousal linking with bone-deep craving and the clenching tightness in her pelvis to combine in a rapturous rush of pleasure that sent her careening into space, splintering delight shockwaving through every sense.

'Wow…' she framed in the aftermath, weighted to the mattress like a stone statue out of its element, gazing up at him with stunned eyes. 'Didn't know I could feel like that.'

'Didn't know I *could* make a woman feel like that,' Rafiq traded with a flashing grin of satisfaction. 'I'm experimenting with you.'

'I'm like a session in the lab? Homework?'

'Infinitely more exciting than that,' Rafiq breathed, sliding between her spread thighs and lowering his head to snatch a breathtakingly demanding kiss that sent her fingers diving into his silky black hair to hold him close.

He surged into her, her body stretching to send sublime messages of pleasure through her quivering length. 'Do that again,' she said raggedly, struggling to breathe.

And he *did*.

And it was even more amazing because he slowed his pace to tease her, sending sensation slowly, oh, so slowly, sending her every nerve-ending into screaming overdrive to the height of excitement and craving. He flipped her over like a rag doll, ground into her from behind at the same time as he strummed that tender bud, and that fast she hit another orgasm, shrieking his name, out of her head, out of control, almost frightened by the drowning onslaught of sheer physical pleasure.

'So, no more separate bedrooms,' Rafiq murmured raggedly as she lay in his arms afterwards. 'Waste of time. Waste of opportunity. Waste of everything that we can be.'

'But we still have an end date,' she reminded him helplessly.

'Everything has an end date,' Rafiq qualified, deciding then and there that he would do everything within his power to stave off that end date for as long as was humanly possible.

'True.' And it was only sex, *casual* sex, she reminded herself, nothing that she needed to get all worked up about. It didn't matter that she didn't know anything about having a casual relationship because presumably he *did* and a few months down the road, she would barely remember him or the ecstasy, she told herself fiercely.

She was young and she was strong, no man's patsy, no man's fool. She would move on, write off Rafiq to the accident of fate he had been. She couldn't call him a mistake because it wasn't his fault that she had conceived, but they didn't belong together. He was going to be a king, for goodness' sake, utterly removed from her in every way, just as their twins would be in their relation to him, she registered belatedly, titled royals with a commoner mother with no claim to fame.

Long powerful fingers splayed across her stomach, which was no longer quite flat. 'I still think they're a miracle,' he murmured levelly. 'And I'm already so curious about them.'

'I suppose you're hoping for a boy to be your heir,' Izzy remarked, involuntarily touched by that miracle reference coming her way again.

'The firstborn will be my heir. Gender is irrelevant. A warrior queen here in the eighteenth century put that kind of sexism behind us. A future queen in waiting will be as acceptable as a king.'

'A *warrior* queen?' Izzy exclaimed, startled by that news.

'And reputedly a tougher negotiator than all the tribal heads put together!' Rafiq extended with amusement. 'It is many years since there was a constitutional bar to a woman taking the throne in Zenara. Zenara may strike you as a conservative country but, in some fields, we've always been quite free thinking.'

That assurance was a huge surprise to Izzy and not an entirely welcome one because in the back of her mind she had already been guilty of thinking that if she gave birth to two girls Rafiq might choose to be less involved with them and seek less regular access. Her cheeks coloured with shame at that ungenerous thought because it *was* selfish of her to want to keep the parental sharing to the minimum. Their children would benefit most from having *two* interested parents.

'Are you planning to visit the children here on weekends and school holidays?' Rafiq enquired curiously, wondering and in great surprise at himself if it could even be vaguely possible to run a marriage on such a part-time basis.

And Izzy froze as if a fire alarm had gone off and sat up with a sudden jerk, a befuddled expression stamping her triangular face as she shook her

head. 'Visit them…*here*?' she repeated in disbelief. 'Why would I be *visiting* my children when
they'll be *living* with me?'

A silence laden with electric undertones fell and
Rafiq gazed back at her with much of the same
frowning disbelief.

'I mean, I know we never actually talked about
the arrangements in any *detail* but I naturally just
a-assumed,' Izzy stammered, watching the dark
tension clench his lean, devastatingly handsome
features taut with a sense of foreboding.

Rafiq was very still. 'And I assumed that you
would be leaving the children here in Zenara with
me to be raised as royals,' he breathed in a raw undertone. 'I thought you understood the situation. It
is not solely of my choosing that they should live
here but how else can they learn the language and
how to integrate with our life if they only make
occasional visits?'

Izzy had already heard more than enough. She
snaked out of the bed like an electrified eel, stooping in haste to gather up her discarded clothing.
Her hands snatched at her panties in desperation
and she struggled to climb into them. Her hands
were shaking. She could not credit, *refused* to
credit that he could have thought for one moment
that she would be prepared to walk out on her

children with only occasional visits back to see them on offer.

'What sort of a monster do you think I am that I could agree to walk away from my kids?' she demanded wrathfully.

Lean, strong face hardening, Rafiq also left the bed. 'I did not attach such an offensive label to you. This is an emotive subject and you need to calm down.'

'I don't need to do anything I don't want to do!' Izzy slammed back at him furiously, outraged to register that she was on the brink of tears.

'Izzy.'

'You made horrible assumptions about me and got me to marry you on false pretences!' she condemned in gritty interruption. 'When I leave Zenara in a few months' time I will be *taking* my children with me!'

'Not without my consent,' Rafiq slung back at her without hesitation as he hauled up his jeans and zipped them.

Izzy froze. She was in a mood, fit to be tied, wholly unable to rationalise the rage and hurt and sense of threat she was experiencing and that declaration of his was the last straw. 'Not…without… *your*…consent?' she questioned incredulously.

'Not without *my* consent,' Rafiq repeated with unapologetic emphasis.

'Well, we'll just see about that!' Izzy flung back wildly, dragging open the door between their rooms and slamming it shut again with a thunderous crash.

CHAPTER EIGHT

'YOU CAN'T JUST get into bed and ignore this!' Rafiq raked down at her as she lay in her bed.

Izzy spared him a brief glance that couldn't quite contrive to take in all of him for, clad only in jeans, a shirt hanging open on his bronzed torso and with his feet still bare, there was an awful lot of tall, lethally well-built Rafiq to encompass.

Izzy parted her lips. 'Watch me,' she urged curtly.

Rafiq stalked across the room like a predator ready to spring on prey and she watched even though she didn't want to. Something about that fluid prowling, loose-limbed grace of his tugged at her every sense and, gritting her teeth, she turned over and buried her hot face in the pillow. She was a mess of conflicting feelings. Rage and hurt. Lust and self-loathing. Fear and resentment.

'We *have* to talk about it,' Rafiq grated.

'Nothing to talk about,' Izzy said mutinously.

'We're not going to take a twin each and call it quits, are we? And since no sane parent would *do* that to their children that leaves us standing in conflicting corners.'

Rafiq flung back the sheet covering her and she flipped over in disbelief, her sapphire eyes alight with fury. He scooped her up, ignoring her struggles, and planted her down on the side of the bed.

'We *will* talk about this,' he said again fiercely.

Bridling like a cat that had been stroked the wrong way, Izzy smoothed a hand down over the silk and lace sleep shorts and strappy top she had put on, uneasily aware of how much skin she was exposing.

'How could you think for one minute that I would walk away from my babies?' she demanded rawly.

'I spent my formative years with a mother who continually walked away. Yes, I saw other maternal examples, in my uncle's home in particular, but I have always been aware that, just as there are men who can walk away from their children, there are also women who choose to do the same thing,' Rafiq completed in a driven undertone.

Izzy could not argue with that statement, but she still flung her head back to look at him, unable to accept that explanation for his assumption about her. 'But you *know* me. I can't believe that you thought *I* would do that.'

'You said you wanted your life back the way it had been. When you married me, you were very set on retaining your freedom and the choices you had already made. I can understand that out-look,' Rafiq conceded grimly. 'It was not for me to judge you.'

'Oh, don't come over all tactful now!' Izzy in-terrupted angrily. 'You assumed that I would give up my children pretty much completely to do… *what*? Train as a teacher? My children are more important and if you don't get that, you don't get anything about me!'

'It may be that I *was* guilty of wishful thinking, of hoping that there would not be conflict between us over this issue.'

'Oh, you'd better believe that there's going to be conflict!' Izzy hissed.

'But there were no false pretences,' Rafiq in-sisted. 'There *was* a genuine misunderstanding. I took too much for granted when you agreed to marry me. I was too keen to persuade you to marry me for the sake of the children, too relieved by your agreement to go into the matter in proper depth. Neither of us clearly expressed our wishes or intentions.'

'It should've been obvious to you that I always intended to take my children back to the UK *with* me.'

Rafiq raised a lean brown hand in an infuriating silencing motion. 'They are *my* children too.'

'I'm their mother,' Izzy stated vehemently.

'And I am their father. Why should I be any more willing to be deprived of my children than you are?' Rafiq demanded wrathfully, stunning dark golden eyes ablaze with anger.

'I wasn't planning to deprive you of them. You would've been free to see them any time you liked!' Izzy fired back.

'And how much time do you think I have to travel to the UK?' Rafiq prompted. 'In eighteen months, I will be King. My uncle only leaves Zenara for state visits, which are tightly scheduled, and he has little free time for travel. I will no longer be travelling on business. Even now I am bound to a very tight itinerary. I am not and I will *not* be free to do as I like.'

Izzy breathed in deep and threw her head back, copper curls dancing around her porcelain-pale face. 'I'm sorry if that is the case but, considering that we agreed to separate before we married, your problems are not *my* problems,' she declared, suppressing the guilt his arguments had unleashed inside her and the sensation that she was being unfair. 'And if you are likely to be *that* busy, surely the children will be much better off living with me.'

'For them I will make time, I will *always* make time,' Rafiq framed with fierce conviction. 'Probably because few people made time for me as a child.'

And her heart clenched inside her because she knew that he would make that effort, knew it for sure even while still furiously, bitterly resenting his willingness to believe that she would have been prepared to accept only an infrequent role acting as a mother to her children.

'This pregnancy may not have been planned but, now that it has happened, I'm fully willing to change and adapt,' she told him curtly.

Rafiq thrust impatient long fingers through the black hair still tousled by her clutching hands. Her face flamed and she looked hurriedly away from him as if by so doing she could block such thoughts and memories.

'It's too late in the day for this conversation,' Rafiq murmured flatly. 'I can see that I have offended you and that was not my intention. Perhaps tomorrow we will both be in a more reasonable state of mind.'

'I still don't understand how we're going to work anything out when we both want the same thing,' Izzy breathed tightly.

'We'll work it out because we're both adults,' Rafiq countered impatiently. 'And adults negotiate and compromise.'

Izzy almost urged him to speak for himself because she wasn't in the mood to compromise, not when it came to being a mother to her own children. That wasn't negotiable, was it? In that field, she wasn't prepared to make concessions because she couldn't afford to bend. It would break her heart to walk away from her babies and deny them her full love and attention. How could he think otherwise?

'I won't surrender my rights,' she whispered tightly as Rafiq reached the connecting door that separated their bedrooms.

Rafiq skimmed dark golden eyes back to her in an electrifying moment of silent communication. 'We'll see.'

No, we won't see, she told herself as she punched her pillow and got back into bed. She wasn't about to change her mind, no matter what he had to say. Some wedding night, she thought prosaically, cringing at the recollection of the intimacy they had shared before she realised how he saw her. Well, monster *was* an exaggeration, she conceded grudgingly, but Rafiq certainly did view her as less than the feminine ideal of caring motherhood and that had bitten deep. Why had it hurt so much? Why on earth did she care so intensely about *his* opinion of her? Why was she so vulnerable when it came to him? Why couldn't she grow a thicker skin?

In the morning she was heavy-eyed and still at odds with herself. It was both a relief and an annoyance to walk out into the courtyard where breakfast was to be served and be greeted with an apology on Rafiq's behalf and the news that a major fire in a hotel in the capital city, Hayad, had demanded his presence early that morning. Braced to see him again and deprived of the expectation, she stiffened and her back went rigid. She would be much happier without him, she told herself staunchly.

She was still deep in that uneasy mood when a young man strolled out from under the trees shading the table. He extended a confident hand in greeting. 'May I join you for breakfast? I'm Rafiq's brother, Zayn.'

Momentarily, Izzy froze because in the midst of all the drama she had forgotten about his visit. But there he was, tall, lean and as dark as Rafiq in col-

ouring and unmistakeably her husband's sibling.
Dark eyes inspected her with unhidden interest.

'I had to see for myself if you could live up to
Uncle Jalil's acclaim,' he admitted as he gave a nod
to a hovering servant and smiled with Rafiq's easy
charm while breakfast arrived at full tilt, offered
in a bedazzling choice of dishes.

'Acclaim?' Izzy queried with a look of surprise.

'My uncle believes that you are exactly what
my brother needs. Considering that he once believed that Fadith was the perfect wife for Rafiq,
who can blame me for being a complete cynic and
refusing to trust in his assessment?'

'Fadith,' Izzy echoed uncomfortably, now
feeling very much under scrutiny, for Rafiq's kid
brother was making no attempt to hide his scepti-
cism. 'Rafiq rarely mentions her.'

'Rafiq never rats on anyone. It's a point of hon-
our for him. An amazing trait for someone who
was shafted at birth and cursed to pay for our late,
unlamented father's sins,' Zayn continued with
bite. 'He deserves better now.'

'Yes,' Izzy agreed, dry-mouthed, feeling under
fire and unsure how to respond with anything
other than honesty. 'And you want to know if I'm
a better bet, but I'm afraid only Rafiq could answer that question.'

'You think?' Zayn lifted a black brow and scoffed, '*Twins?* My brother already thinks you are the eighth wonder of the world!'

Izzy reddened and continued to carefully eat the muesli she had selected. She was tempted to tell Zayn that no woman wanted to be valued purely for her fertility but that was too private a thought for sharing. 'Lucky me,' she murmured a shade flatly.

'Do you love him?'

Izzy glanced across the table in consternation. 'You can't ask me that!'

'I just did. I want my brother to be happy. It's that simple,' Zayn declared unrepentantly.

Feeling under pressure, Izzy pushed her curls back from her damp brow. 'I don't know how I feel. Everything's happened so fast. One minute I was single, the next I was married and expecting twins, for goodness' sake! I've hardly had time to catch my breath.'

'So, that's a no, then,' Zayn assumed, his mouth down curving.

Izzy looked back down at her plate, struggling to concentrate. In truth she didn't know what she felt for Rafiq, only that she felt *too* much in too many different ways, not all of which made sense. Last night, he had left her feeling angry and hurt, but she had still come down to breakfast with a helpless sense of anticipation. The disappointment that had infiltrated her once she learnt of his absence still rang like a hollow bell of warning inside her, reminding her that she couldn't afford to get too attached to the man she had married, not when their marriage wasn't expected to last.

'It's a marriage of convenience,' she told Zayn baldly since he had been so blunt with her. 'And it's early days for us.'

'Only my unlucky brother would get to make *two* marriages of convenience,' Zayn ground out and, glancing at her, he saw her surprise and curiosity. 'No, it wasn't a teenage love match with Fadith. But you need to ask him for the details.'

'I wasn't going to ask you,' Izzy said, thinking *I so was*, her face colouring afresh. Like most people she preferred to avoid contentious issues and it was obvious to her that Rafiq didn't want to talk about his first marriage. Getting the story from Zayn would have been easier, most particularly when she and Rafiq were currently at daggers drawn.

Evidently accepting that he had got all he was likely to get from her, Zayn engaged in normal conversation for what remained of the meal. He was much less guarded than his older brother, yet very mature for his age, only his sudden boyishly enthusiastic smile betraying his youth. She understood his loyal protectiveness towards Rafiq because she was equally attached to her twin and two orphaned brothers, regardless of the age gap between them, were almost certain to be close.

They sat in the shade playing poker, Izzy working up a tally of losses that hugely amused Zayn.

'It's lucky for you that we agreed not to play for money,' he teased. 'You're a hopeless card player.'

'It's been a long time since I played,' Izzy admitted ruefully.

'I'd take you for a drive in the desert but Rafiq thinks I'm reckless at the wheel and you're too precious a cargo for me to take the risk,' he told her cheerfully.

They ended up playing a board game then, which Zayn played with the same ferocious spirit of competitiveness. When he departed in a helicopter before lunch, he and Izzy were on easy terms and she was sorry to see him leave. After lunch she felt queasy and went for a nap, but it didn't help. Her pregnant stomach was determined to be oversensitive and feeling under par was a side effect she assumed she had to accept. It was a surprise when a doctor was shown in by her maid, who had evidently contacted him. Where he had come from, she had no idea and she was taken aback to be told when she asked that he was the doctor 'in residence' at Alihreza. A herbal tea was prescribed and Izzy sipped it throughout the afternoon, pleasantly disconcerted to discover that it did definitely help the nausea and reduced it to a more bearable level.

She dozed through the hottest hours of the day, wakening to learn that Rafiq was on his way back. She went for a shower to freshen up, enjoying the cool sprays hitting her overheated skin before rifling through her new wardrobe to pick a casual cotton blue-and-white maxi dress that was both cool and comfortable. It was unnerving how fast her body was changing, she thought ruefully. Her breasts had swelled at least a cup size and her once neat waist was vanishing as her stomach pushed out.

When she heard another helicopter flying in, she was reading a magazine in the shade of the courtyard. Eventually, Rafiq came striding across the courtyard towards her and by that stage she was seriously tense and mentally walking on eggshells.

Sheathed in jeans and an open shirt, his bronzed skin shadowed by stubble, his stunning eyes gleaming at her from between lush lashes, Rafiq was a lethally lustrous and rawly masculine presence. Instantly her senses went on high alert, her heart rate increasing and, that quickly, she wanted to slap herself until she wised up. It was one thing to be attracted to the man she had married, quite another to break out in a girlish fever just because she was seeing him for the first time that day.

'My uncle sends his profuse apologies for dragging me back to Hayad for the day and leaving you alone here.'

'The fire…was it serious?'

Rafiq nodded grimly. 'A club popular with our young people. Although there were few deaths, many serious injuries were caused by the panic that broke out once the alarms and the sprinklers went off. I have been dealing with distraught parents and fire officials all day,' he confided heavily, studying her with appreciation. 'It is a relief to come back here and find you sitting calmly beneath the trees looking as fresh as a daisy.'

'But not feeling calm,' she muttered awkwardly, never able to be comfortable accepting a compliment and cringing because that made her feel as gauche as an adolescent.

'I understand that Dr Karim needed to attend you this afternoon.'

'Yes and he's very charming,' Izzy responded with a stiff smile. 'Why is there a resident doctor?'

'Because you're here and my uncle is very mindful of your health and keen to ensure that, should there be any kind of emergency, expert care is on hand,' he admitted. 'But while the doctor is here, he is also treating the staff and the local Bedouin. He will have a constant procession of patients requesting his attention.'

Izzy relaxed a little more and watched Rafiq take a seat opposite her, the sheer vibrancy of him that close tugging at her with invisible cords.

Rafiq drank in the sight of her, as pretty as a picture, and swiftly looked away again, troubled by the shuttered look in her once clear eyes and her defensive posture. He was responsible for that change in her, he reminded himself broodingly. She no longer trusted him. He had made a huge error with his assumptions and destroyed any faith she had had in him. He had screwed up royally and now he had to redress the damage at the same time as he concentrated on achieving the end goal *he* wanted.

'Now, tell me,' he urged. 'Are you well?'

His air of gravity made her frown. 'It was only a bit of sickness, Rafiq, nothing serious, nothing unexpected. Please don't fuss over me. I'm young, strong and healthy.'

'I don't see concern as fussing,' Rafiq countered. 'Obviously, I will worry about your well-being. I am keenly aware that what we discussed last night was destructive. Now you don't trust me. You may even fear that I could be planning to try and take our children from you.'

Izzy turned pale at that suggestion and goose-flesh cooled her arms as fright gripped her. 'No, I hadn't got quite that far yet but I don't want to even hear you *say* such a thing.'

'Fears voiced aloud cause less concern than those that remain secret and unspoken,' Rafiq murmured. 'I don't want you worrying about anything at the moment. Stress is bad for you.'

'Stress is an integral part of being temporarily married to and pregnant by a...a stranger,' Izzy muttered in an apologetic rush. 'You don't *feel* like a stranger to me. Somehow you never did but how much do I really know about you and what you could, ultimately, be capable of? And where do we go from here?'

Disconcertingly when she least expected it, Rafiq smiled, a flashing charismatic smile that warmed her chilled and anxious body from the inside out. 'We will work it out, Izzy. I promise you that we will work it out without any harm or hurt to anyone,' he assured her.

His sheer confidence blasted out at her like a force field, the controlled power of the nature he hid behind a cool, measured facade lacing his stunning dark eyes and flawless masculine features as he studied her.

'That's a lovely idea but I don't think it will prove possible in the long run,' Izzy countered heavily. 'We're going to fight—'

'We are *not* going to fight,' Rafiq sliced in with conviction as she shifted, the hem of her dress lifting to reveal delicate ankles wrapped in impossibly feminine ribbon ties. It was the ribbons that he found sexy, he told himself, unable to imagine any ribbon attached to Izzy's body that he wouldn't want to tug loose and untie. Hardening, he shifted position, regretting his tight jeans. 'I may have been apart from you today but, believe me, I didn't waste my time. I considered all our options and we have many more than you seem to think.'

'Options?' Izzy repeated, her brow furrowing. 'Like maybe…we separate now before everything gets even more complicated?'

His dense spiky lashes dipped to screen his gaze and he almost swore in frustration at that startling suggestion. 'That definitely wasn't one of my options,' he admitted.

Her attention lingered on his full sensual mouth, framed and accentuated as it was by a blue black shadow of stubble. A hot liquid sensation tugged in her pelvis and she pressed her thighs together, sudden painfully intense hunger gripping her like a dangerous drug. 'Well, what was…er…*your* preferred option?' she prompted, dry-mouthed, so tense that she couldn't even swallow.

The silence simmered like a haze of heat on a hot day, blurring her surroundings and the clarity of her thoughts but fully centring her attention on him.

'Easier than yours… I think,' Rafiq husked, springing upright with that lithe, fluid grace that stabbed her with a longing she could not control.

'Easier?' she questioned breathlessly.

Without the smallest warning, Rafiq bent down and scooped her up off the padded sofa into his arms. A startled sound of surprise was wrenched from her and she gazed up at him with huge sapphire-blue eyes. 'Rafiq…what are you doing?'

'What comes most naturally to me,' he murmured, settling back on his seat to cradle her across his lean muscular thighs, his arms caging her in place. 'You chose a pessimistic option. *I* choose a more positive one.'

'Oh…?' she gasped, heart hammering, body striving to melt into the pure heated allure of him that close in spite of her attempt to remain stiff and discouraging.

'We continue as we are,' Rafiq breathed in hoarse extension. 'Last night wasn't planned. Nothing that has happened between us has been planned. The attraction is too powerful to be ignored and too rare to be discounted or suppressed.'

'A-attraction? *Rare?*' Izzy exclaimed, sapphire eyes welded to glowing gold.

'I have never wanted any woman as much as I want you,' Rafiq confirmed without hesitation.

'You said…*continue* as we are?'

'Give our marriage a decent chance while we await the birth of our children,' Rafiq extended. 'We see if we can make it work and if *we* work, we stay together to raise our family.'

'You mean…like a *real* marriage?' she almost whispered as he stroked his fingertips across a slender ribbon-bound ankle.

Beautiful dark golden eyes held hers fast and hard. 'I want to keep you *and* our children but there are still other variations on the same theme available, which, if you wish, we can discuss. I am prepared to be flexible.'

His hand was sliding up her calf and she was lost in the sensations darting to more tender areas of her body. Indeed, the stroke of his knowing fingers against the sensitive soft skin of her inner thigh fired up every sense. That fast she wanted to rip off his shirt and sink down on the male arousal pushing boldly against her hip. Her face flamed. Rafiq brought out every shameless urge she possessed, introducing her to a side of herself she had not known existed until he appeared in her life.

Variations on the same theme, though, God bless him, she thought helplessly, her soft mouth quirking, recognising that he had approached her armed with every possibility he could muster, like a businessman engaged in trying to finalise a very important deal.

He didn't know how to do romantic, didn't even try. *But* without a doubt he wanted to *keep* her, and that truth smashed down Izzy's barriers and flooded through her defences to wash them away. The craving inside her, which she had been fighting to the very last ditch, was released like a sudden storm. Without a single word, she snaked up her hand to spear her fingers into his luxuriant black hair to drag his beautiful sensual mouth down to hers.

His lips smashed down on hers with an urgency that thrilled her to the marrow of her bones. He wanted her, he desired her as no man had ever desired or wanted her and, in that moment, the simple knowledge that he wanted her as much as she wanted him was sufficient to silence every other insecurity. Rafiq was going to be hers, absolutely hers for ever, because she wasn't prepared to let him go. His tongue plunged deep into the damp interior of her mouth and she moaned low in her throat.

'Dinner will be late tonight,' Rafiq breathed raggedly as he leapt up with her still clutched in his arms and strode towards the lift below the arches. 'Very, *very* late.'

Her entire body still buzzing from the provocative stroke of his fingers, Izzy was simply out of her mind with the same desire that powered him. Only he had the nerve that she lacked, she acknowledged, burying her hot face in a wide strong shoulder as he stalked past the servants hovering on the terrace, unconcerned by their scrutiny, unashamed of his passion. In the lift, he pinned her against the mirrored wall and kissed her breathless and she rocked against him like a shameless hussy, craving the arousal he couldn't hide from her, needing that physical contact in that instant as much as she needed air to breathe.

'You're amazing,' he told her thickly, laying her down across his bed. 'The most amazing woman I've ever met.'

It's only sex, her brain warned her, but she silenced that voice at supersonic speed because she was living in the moment—*revelling* in the moment, if truth be told—as Rafiq stood back and stripped, all urgency and hunger and appreciation, revealing a lean bronzed torso taut with muscle definition, exposing long powerful hair-roughened thighs.

It didn't get better than this, she told herself dizzily, it would *never* get better than this...

CHAPTER NINE

THE FOLLOWING DAY at Alihreza, Rafiq rose early, kissed her brow and headed for his office to catch up on work.

Izzy lay in bed feeling exceedingly foolish for her complete capitulation the night before. Her intelligence hadn't featured much in that decision, she acknowledged with a wince. Reality was, however, now staring her in the face. She was falling in love with Rafiq. What had started out as an infatuation had transformed into something much deeper and more long lasting. The instant he had offered her the chance to stay and become a normal wife rather than a temporary one, she had snatched at the offer, hadn't even hung back long enough to ask to hear the *other* options. She raised cooling hands to her hot face and groaned in chagrin.

She had agreed to stay married to a man who didn't love her and who would probably never love her. A man already familiar with the limits of a marriage of convenience, a man whose sole driving interest was in retaining custody of his unborn children. There it was: the awful truth she didn't want to face. Rafiq's primary objective was keeping his heir and spare in Zenara and raising them in his own home. She was a prized incubator to be tended, not a woman with thoughts and needs of her own. Realistically, Rafiq was likely to tell her whatever it took to keep her in Zenara. And how did that bode for their future? Or her happiness? Could she settle for that?

'Of course, you can't settle for that,' her sister told her sternly on the phone an hour later. 'I'll be flying in to see you in a few weeks.'

'The plane fares to Zenara cost a fortune!' Izzy warned her twin.

Maya laughed but it was an almost bitter laugh that made Izzy frown because she didn't get the joke. 'Money's not a problem for me now,' her sister declared. 'We have a lot to catch up on but I'm concentrating on the fact that I've settled Mum and Dad's problems for all time and no sacrifice is too great to achieve that, is it?'

'If you're the sacrifice, I'm not sure,' Izzy sighed. 'Oh, Maya, do you truly *hate* this job?'

'It's not a typical job. We'll talk when I see you. Face to face is always better.'

But the weeks passed and in the end Maya wasn't able to visit. First, she fell ill and said she didn't want Izzy to visit her in Italy, which hurt but had to be accepted. And then in the aftermath she said she didn't feel either like travelling or entertaining and that had to be accepted too, Izzy conceding that for the very first time her twin was asking for space from her. Maybe it was part of growing up and attaining adult independence, she reasoned worriedly, wondering if she had been coming across as a little too clingy and demanding in the sibling stakes while resolving to let Maya get on with forging her own path.

In the meantime, life went on in Zenara. Izzy was able to satisfy her curiosity about Rafiq's first marriage as he began talking more freely to her. 'The guilt after Fadith's death was the worst burden.' Rafiq sighed, smoothing long fingers over the firm swell of Izzy's pregnant stomach as they lay in bed a few weeks later. 'In truth the marriage was miserable for both of us. Fadith never attained what she most desired…a child or even the status of Queen.'

'Was that so important to her?' Izzy queried, running a hand down over his flat, taut stomach to stroke him with tender possessive fingertips and smile as he stretched and groaned half under his breath, loving the effect she could have on him. 'I mean, I can understand her desire for a child, particularly when the two of you were hoping for an heir to the throne, but I don't really understand why being Queen was so important.'

'Because that was why she married me. Status meant a lot to her and her family.'

'I can't understand that outlook.'

'No, but then you're different, wonderfully different,' Rafiq growled, rolling her over to pin her beneath him. 'Fadith never loved me, never wanted me for me. A passionate clandestine romance with one of her brother's friends before our marriage set that in stone. He died in a car crash and she decided that she'd never love again, which is why she agreed to marry me.'

'So, she wasn't a virgin,' Izzy remarked in surprise.

'No but she was honest enough to tell me that before I agreed to marry her. I was shocked, out of my depth because I was much more naïve than she was and although virginity isn't demanded, it is rather taken for granted in a marriage at our level. Girls are sheltered, guarded in our society,' Rafiq confided. 'I was more surprised that she had loved someone else.'

'Oh, dear,' Izzy whispered reflectively. 'That was far too much for you to take on at sixteen.'

'I wasn't jealous because she felt more like a sister to me than a wife for months after we married,' Rafiq admitted wryly. 'That brought problems too. All she ever really seemed to want from me was a baby and, sadly, when she didn't achieve motherhood she blamed me for it. She was totally convinced that if there was anything wrong with either of us, it had to be *my* problem, my flaw.'

Izzy winced, imagining what that must've been like for them both when the expected development failed to materialise over ten long years. 'For me, babies were always something I knew I wanted but it was also something that was planned for way in the distant future,' she told him absently. 'But now that it's something very much in the present, I've adjusted.'

They had moved back to the royal palace outside Hayad and Rafiq had taken up his usual duties, taking her with him on official activities when it was appropriate to do so. After a couple of engagements at schools, Izzy found herself becoming interested in the education system and she agreed to take those visits on. A second ultrasound revealed that she was carrying two girls. She flew over to London twice to visit her family with Rafiq by her side and found her parents and her little brother hale and hearty, her father talking with enthusiasm about some new sales job he had managed to get. The visit, however, had been dominated by Izzy needing to come clean and explain to her family who Rafiq was and that they were married. She told Maya on the phone, where Maya dropped her own marriage bombshell, telling Izzy about a whirlwind romance with her new Italian boss. Something in Maya's story didn't quite sit right with Izzy, but Maya deflected her twin's worried questioning, choosing instead to concentrate on Izzy's own news.

As her pregnancy advanced, the nausea vanished but Izzy went out less, aside from a short trip back to the UK to spend a weekend with Maya and her new husband and their extended family. The fact was that Izzy was embarrassed by her increasingly cumbersome body. Her beautiful cunningly shaped maternity clothes could only do so much and she still thought she most closely resembled a barrel because a twin pregnancy on her slight frame was enormous. Rafiq might tell her that she was 'glowing' but she couldn't find it within her heart to quite believe his sincerity and when her ankles swelled up unattractively, and even her face began to show the same tendency, the doctors advised more rest and she did exactly as she was told.

Rafiq was wonderfully supportive every step
of the way. He did not leave her alone for longer
than a night, but she felt increasingly less desirable as her pregnancy progressed and the doctors
warned them that, with her rising blood pressure
and other symptoms, sex was best taken off the
menu until the delivery of their twins was safely
accomplished. Rafiq acted as if the bar on the
seething passion that had once united them was
no great loss and she blamed his easy acceptance
on her swollen stomach, assuming that he no longer found her quite so attractive.

No longer, however, did she kid herself about
her own feelings. She adored Rafiq and, although
it embarrassed her, it was still a struggle to keep
her hands off him. He still shared a bed with her
every night, and she cherished that intimacy, loving the way he still held her close even when she
complained, tongue in cheek, that he made her too
warm. While they had still been lovers, she had felt
needed by him, necessary, *desired*. Without that
physical connection, she felt bereft, unimportant,
insignificant aside of the reality that she was carrying their children.

Did he feel anything for her at all, beyond the
reality that his children's well-being rested on
hers? Was her only value to him based on her

ability to bring the twins into the world? What about her personally? Was there another dimension to his care of her, beyond that of her pregnancy? Those were the fears that tormented Izzy with every passing day.

She studied the ever-growing collection of her jewellery and picked sapphires to wear over diamonds. Earlier in life it could never have occurred to her that such luxurious choices would one day be hers. But Rafiq's generosity and frequent gifts had endowed her with a fabulous collection of priceless jewels. She donned a pair of loose flowing pants with a tunic and high heels, reckoning that she would look like a ship in full sail but aware that she had no real choice in the clothes department, having developed a girth that normal garments could not encompass.

Rafiq was always giving her stuff but the superb nursery being put together down the corridor in a previously unused section of the palace was even more telling. She had picked a bright jungle print and primary colours to provide their twins with a stimulating decor. Rafiq had taken an interest in every single choice she made, unashamedly enthralled by the prospect of being a father. His enthusiasm both warmed her heart and hurt her at the same time. If only he could have focused that emotional intensity on *her*…and why shouldn't she *ask* him where she stood in his life? What was she so afraid of? If all he cared about was the babies she carried, she had the right to know that and he would probably be honest enough to tell her. So, she would *ask*…

She was about to leave her bedroom when a cramp gripped her stomach and she fell still, her hand pressing against her abdomen. When a damp sensation assailed her, she rushed into the bathroom to check herself. Horror gripped her when she saw the bright red blood.

Oh, dear heaven, was she losing her babies? She had believed she was safe this far on in her pregnancy—well, as safe as any woman could ever be in her condition. In a panic, she stabbed the button on the household line that would summon Dr Karim…

CHAPTER TEN

EVERYTHING THAT HAPPENED over the next hour was ever after a blur for Izzy.

Dr Karim came running and then she was being swept off in an ambulance, Rafiq hanging onto her hand, as pale as someone of his bronzed complexion could be. He looked like a man in the grip of his worst nightmare and, ridiculously, she wanted to smooth his tumbled black hair from his brow and soothe him.

'We're going to deliver the babies now,' Dr Karim told her gently, after she had been separated from Rafiq and a nurse had helped to undress her and slot her into a hospital gown. 'But I'm afraid it will be a C-section, because one of the babies has moved into a breech position.'

'It's too early!' Izzy gasped, stricken, frantically worrying about the survival of her twins.

Mr Abbas, the English-speaking consultant obstetrician engaged for her delivery, whom she had already met on several occasions, joined them and answered her.

'No, it is only a couple of weeks early and we were prepared for this development by your most recent ultrasound. We have every prospect of achieving a safe delivery,' he declared with immense confidence as she was wheeled into the operating theatre and monitors were attached to her. The epidural was administered without any pain.

Rafiq reappeared by her side, gowned and masked, his lean, darkly handsome features rigid with fierce tension.

'Mr Abbas…' Rafiq urged half under his breath. 'Whatever happens, my wife must come through this procedure safely. *She* must be your first priority.'

Izzy blinked rapidly, her eyes dazed, because she was certain she had to have either misheard or misunderstood that instruction.

'Try to relax, Your Royal Highness, I fully intend to bring all three of your family safely through this experience,' Mr Abbas informed him as the doors of the theatre swung open and an entire medical team trooped in to join them and a series of checks was carried out.

Rafiq squeezed the life out of her hand. He looked terrified.

'A lot of women have to have this,' Izzy felt it incumbent on her to state.

'This is you,' Rafiq rebutted hoarsely. 'There is only one you.'

A sheet was erected, cutting off her view of her lower body. Her fingers went numb in Rafiq's fierce hold. She felt that she was being touched and then there was a little pressure but absolutely no pain. What seemed like only a few minutes later a baby's wail broke through the silence and a cross little face topped with a shock of dark hair appeared for an instant before disappearing again.

'That's Leila,' Izzy whispered in total awe.

'She's...' Words seemed to fail Rafiq entirely at that point.

'And that's Lucia,' Izzy added when a second baby made a brief appearance above the sheet.

She wasn't able to hold them. The operating theatre was too cold for them and the babies had to be checked and wrapped up warm to be borne off. As she turned to comment on the fact to Rafiq, there was a crashing sound and she caught a narrow glimpse of him sprawled on the floor before aides rushed to lift him and help him out.

'He will be fine, Your Royal Highness,' Mr Abbas murmured gently. 'The emergency was a little too much for your husband's nerves. The

Crown Prince has been very concerned throughout your pregnancy.'

'Has he?' Izzy muttered in surprise, because she genuinely hadn't realised that Rafiq was actively worried, had simply assumed that he viewed caring for the needs of a pregnant wife as his duty and responsibility.

'A not unexpected reaction from a man who saw his mother die after his brother's birth. That delivery was a sadly botched business and I'm sure it left a mark on our future King to have witnessed such a tragedy as a young child.'

She was moved into the recovery room and asked if she required anything for pain. She didn't, and when two nurses came in wheeling tiny cribs that held her babies, she was entranced. Leila had Rafiq's hair and Lucia was blonde, a sort of sandy strawberry blonde that might or might not turn red. Izzy cradled each baby to her in turn and smiled, so very relieved that everything had gone well and quite in awe of her children. When Rafiq appeared in the doorway, still looking pale, she beamed and extended a hand to him encouragingly. 'Come and see them properly,' she urged.

'I'm sorry,' he breathed tautly, his stunning dark golden eyes full of regret. 'I wasn't able to be there for you as I should have been.'

'No, I'm the one who should be apologising,' Izzy told him ruefully. 'It never crossed my mind that you could be so wound up about this.'

'I didn't want to alarm you with my fears. My anxiety was better kept to myself,' Rafiq pointed out stiffly.

'I didn't know that you *saw* your mother die,' she muttered with regret. 'I wish you had told me that.'

'*Not* while you were pregnant. All I could do was ensure that you had the very best medical care available,' he countered gravely. 'And look after you.'

And look after her he *had*, continually fussing over what she ate and how much she rested and how she felt, she acknowledged, reckoning that she had been blind not to suspect the very real fear that he was concealing on her behalf.

'I won't tell anyone that you fainted,' Izzy murmured, reaching out to close a hand over his.

'With the number of staff that witnessed my collapse, it will be a well-told story the length and the breadth of Zenara,' Rafi responded in a wry tone of acceptance. 'I am simply grateful that both my wife and my daughters are safe and healthy.'

'Would you like to hold them now?' Izzy proffered.

Rafiq sank down in the chair beside her bed and Leila was placed in his arms. He studied the tiny face under the pink beany hat and Izzy watched him swallow hard and blink rapidly, but the sheen in his lustrous gaze was unmistakeably emotional. He touched a careful fingertip to her little cupid's bow mouth. 'So tiny…'

'I'll have you know that they are both a very good weight and isn't it wonderful that, even though they've arrived a little early, they don't need to be put in incubators?' Izzy proclaimed with pride. 'We'll be able to take them home with us as soon as we're ready.'

'I would like you to spend two nights here within the care of trained personnel…just to be safe,' Rafiq admitted quietly as Leila was returned to her mother and Lucia was brought to him.

'So precious,' he muttered with deep appreciation. 'I think they are going to have blue eyes and this little lady may even have inherited your hair. My uncle and aunt and Zayn would like to visit this evening. Do you feel up to that? Feel free to ask them to wait until tomorrow.'

'No, I'll be fine. I want to show my daughters off,' Izzy admitted with a rueful grin. 'But I have to phone my own family first.'

'Perhaps I could contact your parents for you,

and you could take care of your sister. I hope that she will come to meet her nieces. I know you have been worrying about her and that you would enjoy that,' he completed thoughtfully.

It was one of those moments when she almost dropped her guard and told him that she loved him but she swallowed the words, recalling the guy who had been trapped for ten years in an unhappy marriage and who had settled, for the sake of his children, for a second loveless marriage without complaint. If she told him how she felt about him, he would feel that once again he wasn't delivering what his wife wanted and needed because he didn't love her back. She couldn't do that to him, she just *couldn't* do that, not when he already made such an effort to be caring and supportive. She must have imagined those instructions he had given the doctor about making her safety a priority during the birth. Surely the children, his heirs, must always have come first on his scale? Obviously she had got it wrong because he could never have uttered such a heresy, she reflected, not when their entire relationship was based on the importance of the babies she had conceived.

Three days later, thoroughly rested, she travelled back to the palace in a limousine flying the Zenarian flag. She showered and dressed slowly, careful of the occasional twinge from the site of the incision and pleased to see that as her stomach receded a hint of a waist was already beginning to show again. The arrival of the twins in the nursery was a real event in the palace because it had been so many years since there had been babies in the royal family. The staff were very excited and flocked to see the little girls.

A week later there were many appreciative sighs over the picture Leila and Lucia made when they were dressed in white broderie-anglaise camera-ready outfits for the official family photograph session that was expected of them. Rafiq argued that it was too soon, and that Izzy needed more time to recover from the birth, but Izzy was well on the road to recovery by then and said she would sooner get the photo call over and done with.

After all, Izzy thought, little was expected of the Zenarian royal family in terms of public exposure and, after the years of scandalous headlines and rumours generated by Rafiq's misbehaving father, the family had all chosen to follow a low-key lifestyle. They were expected to appear at ceremonial occasions and official events, but the private life of the royal family remained private and there were no paparazzi hunting them in the hope of digging up dirt. The birth of the twins, however, fell into the realm of public interest and the populace needed to see the children.

'And their future Queen,' Rafiq reminded Izzy gently as she gave her opinion to him. 'You should put on some jewellery.'

'I'm never going to be able to pull off *regal*,' Izzy opined with a grimace, smoothing down her tailored cream dress while her maid was directed by Rafiq to lay out diamonds for her to put on.

'Your beauty and our children are more than enough to impress,' Rafiq assured her with amusement. 'Leila and Lucia are the next generation of an unbroken line that our people never thought to see continued except through Zayn and that would have required a change in the law.'

The Regent awaited them in the same elegant reception room where their wedding ceremony had been staged. Izzy's daughters delighted her by falling asleep for the session and the photographer was quick to take advantage. Within twenty minutes the photographs were complete, and the twins were being settled back into their cradles.

'You know, you never did tell me what those other options concerning our marriage were,' Izzy remarked as they walked into his bedroom, which had somehow become *their* bedroom, except when she was getting dressed because her wardrobe was stored in her room next door.

Rafiq froze where he stood. 'Why are you asking about those options now?'

'I'm just curious,' she told him truthfully.

Rafiq nodded his proud dark head, his stunning dark golden eyes resting full on her face. 'It's a little late in the day to discuss those options now,' he began tautly.

'Only if you are already taking it for granted that our marriage is working and that I'm going to stay in Zenara for good,' Izzy pointed out defensively.

'You would hold me to ransom now that our children are born?' Rafiq demanded, disconcerting anger flashing in his strained gaze, warning her that he had not been in any way prepared for such a dialogue.

Izzy straightened her slim shoulders. 'It's not a question of holding you to ransom,' she framed with distaste. 'Maybe I think it's time for us to have a conversation about where we go from here. Not talking about it makes me feel like I'm still on trial in the wife stakes!'

Rafiq stared back at her in apparent disbelief. 'How could you ever have thought for one moment

that you were *on trial* with me?' he demanded
rawly.

'Well, isn't that the right label for the way
we've been living for the past few months?' Izzy
prompted tartly, although she was trying hard not
to lose her temper. 'You made the deal. You set the
rules. You said we'd see if we *worked* as a couple
and you've never mentioned the subject since!'

'Evidently I'm no good at making deals or
agreements with you!' Rafiq retorted in a sav-
age undertone. 'I always get it wrong and now
you're asking about the options I referred to at
the time. They were of a more short-term nature
than long-term.'

'I'd still like to know what they were,' Izzy
pressed, seriously unnerved by the storm she had
unleashed with her awkward questions.

Rafiq stalked over to the window, his strong
jaw line clenched hard. 'I could have asked my
uncle for permission to base myself in the UK for
a few months while you followed your teacher-
training course. I would've bought a house there,
but I would have asked you to return to Zenara for
the birth so that our daughters would be born here.'

'OK. That was a…a considerate option,' Izzy
acknowledged, struggling to come up with the

right words in response to that surprise possibility that he had chosen not to share with her at the time.

'Another choice would have entailed you doing your studies here. As you know, we have classes at the university taught in English,' he reminded her doggedly. 'Both options, as I'm sure you have noted, involved us remaining together as a couple. Had the Regent and the executive council refused to agree to my spending so much time abroad, I would have joined you in the UK every weekend instead.'

'So...' Izzy mused thoughtfully, mulling over what he was telling her. 'None of the options let me walk away free and clear.'

His bold, strong profile went rigid and he swung back to her, golden eyes blazing like flames. 'No,' he agreed without apology. 'I wasn't prepared to let you go free and if you'd run away, I would have followed you and endeavoured to persuade you into returning. There is nothing I would not have done to keep you.'

As she listened Izzy's heart was hammering and ridiculous hope was suddenly blossoming inside her tight chest to such an extent that it was a challenge to breathe. 'And why was that?'

'I do not think I could live without you in my life,' Rafiq grated between his teeth, as though the words were being torn from him under the pressure of the cruellest torture. 'You have transformed my life and I will do just about anything not to return to the life I led before I met you. It was empty, joyless. My sole focus was becoming King, and my sole interest was this country. Now…wrong though it is in my position…*you* are my main focus!'

'Well, I don't see what's wrong with that or why you should get so worked up about sharing that with me,' Izzy told him softly. 'I think what you're saying is that you love me.'

'You don't love me when you can ask about those options all these months on!' Rafiq shot at her rawly, his pain and vulnerability palpable to her.

'No, I just wanted to know where I stood and now I know that I'm standing exactly where I want to be,' Izzy murmured gently as she crossed the room to his side. 'Because I love you too. I started falling for you the day we met but you walked away, and I would never have seen you again if I hadn't traced you because I'd fallen pregnant.'

'I wouldn't be so sure of that. Misguided and unwise though it was when I was being expected to take a wife again, I had your name and your address and sooner or later I would have used that information to see you again because I don't believe that I could've stayed away!' he confessed in an emotional surge. 'I wanted you the moment I first saw you and I never stopped wanting you, not for a moment. I didn't even look at another woman after being with you.'

Izzy stretched up tender hands to frame his lean, devastatingly handsome features. 'It was pretty much the same for me. Is that why you said that you believed in fate?'

'Yes, I believe we were fated to meet, fated to be together,' he told her raggedly. 'You really do love me?'

'You're so very easy to love,' she murmured, her heart lurching at the longing, the need for reassurance that she could see in his beautiful eyes, this man, who had known neither the love of his mother nor the love of his first wife, who did not even understand or fully believe that he *could* inspire love in any woman.

His essential humility had fooled her into crediting that he was merely staying married to her to preserve the status quo and keep his heirs in Zenara. How much blinder could she have been not to recognise that a man who still held her all night even when there was no prospect of sexual satisfaction had to truly *care* about her?

'So at the hospital when you said, "There is only one you"—'

'I was admitting that I loved you and that you are irreplaceable,' he proffered tautly. 'I was so scared that something would go wrong, that the staff would automatically prioritise the heir to the throne's survival over yours...should there have been that horrible choice. We could, conceivably, have other children but I could not replace you, the woman I love, with anyone. I have never known such fear.'

'Oh, Rafiq,' she sighed, wrapping both arms around him, rejoicing in the strength of his tall, well-built physique. 'If only you had told me sooner how you felt.'

'My mother and Fadith showed me that women don't appreciate men who get too emotional,' he confided in a tight undertone. 'I didn't want you to think less of me. I didn't want to appear weak in your eyes. Weakness is not an attractive trait and I was trying to win your love.'

'And all the time you already *had* my love,' she whispered with a huge smile bright with happiness. 'Just as I couldn't recognise your feelings, you couldn't recognise mine.'

'I've never been in love before, only in lust, and that only briefly and never with anyone who mat-

tered to me beyond that level. But it was different
with you from the start. I began falling for you the
minute you told me about the guy who wore eye-
liner because nobody ever chats to me about stuff
like that,' he admitted ruefully. 'I loved how natural you were with me. I didn't want to tell you who
I was. I didn't want to walk away from you, but I
wasn't free to do what I wanted. I had promised
my uncle that I would remarry so that Zayn could
have another few years of freedom before being
forced to marry and procreate for my benefit. And
in the light of that promise, it would have been
wrong for me to seek to see you again.'

'And yet you still went to the trouble of finding
out where I lived. How did you find out?'

'I suspect that someone at the rental agency you
worked for was bribed. I didn't ask for the grubby
details. I just wanted the information even though
I knew I was only tempting myself with what I
couldn't have, because seeing you again would
only have made the idea of marrying some other
woman more of a nightmare than it already was.'

Rafiq freed her and strode over to open the safe
in the wall, extracting a small box from it. 'I was
saving this for your twenty-second birthday next
week but now seems more like the right moment,'

he breathed with a flashing smile as he handed the box to her.

Izzy lifted the lid on a glittering diamond eternity ring, and he removed it from its velvet mount and eased it onto her finger with an air of satisfaction. 'It's beautiful,' she whispered appreciatively. 'I love you so much.'

'You fill my heart to overflowing,' Rafiq breathed, stroking his fingers down the side of her heart-shaped face, making her shiver. 'You are everything I never dared to dream of in a woman and a wife. You make me amazingly happy and for the first time I am at peace with the future, content to become King when it is the right time, in no hurry to rush ahead and miss or waste a single moment of being with you and my children.'

Izzy gave him an intoxicated smile and watched the sunlight sparkle a rainbow on her ring. 'You're really very romantic.'

'No, I'm not,' he protested instantly, a tinge of colour scoring his high cheekbones. 'Not at all.'

'Nobody but me needs to know what you're like behind closed doors,' she pointed out softly.

Rafiq brought his mouth down hungrily on hers. 'I'm starving for you!' he groaned, instantly breaking away from her again. 'But we should wait until the doctor has advised us that—'

'Well, we still have a few weeks to wait,' Izzy informed him ruefully, shimmying out of her fancy frock with a tantalising smile to expose curves embellished by silk and lace lingerie. 'But that doesn't mean that we can't do other things,' she pointed out shamelessly.

Rafiq hovered for a split second as if he couldn't quite believe that he was allowed to touch her again and then he stalked forward and lifted her into his arms to kiss her with fierce urgency. 'All those nights we couldn't.'

'All those nights,' she agreed on the back of a sigh of recollection. 'But you held me close anyway and I really loved that about you. I wouldn't have blamed you if you'd shifted me back to my own room.'

'I like being close to you even if I can't make love to you,' he breathed raggedly as he shrugged free of his jacket and tore off his tie with flattering enthusiasm. 'And by the way, you don't *have* your own room any longer.'

Her brow furrowed. 'How don't I?'

'Why would you need your own room? We'll turn it into a dressing room for you. From now on, you will always share my bed. I've got used to having company,' he confided teasingly.

'I suppose I'll always have the sofa to escape to when you annoy me,' Izzy told him playfully.

'And I'll snatch you off it again,' he promised, amusement dancing in his eyes, a new relaxation in his lean, darkly handsome features as he feasted his beautiful eyes on her smiling face. 'I love you, Izzy. I love you like I never thought I could love anyone...'

Silence crept in, broken only by occasional murmurs as discarded garments fell to the floor and they rediscovered each other and the passion that had first brought them together in a blaze of glory that consumed them until the real world crept back in. Izzy realised that it was feeding time for the twins and she needed to put some clothes on again. The buoyant happiness that had flooded her peaked as Rafiq threw on jeans and watched her with loving admiration brightening his keen gaze.

'You and our daughters have become the very centre of my world,' he murmured with satisfaction.

EPILOGUE

Two years later, Izzy hurriedly clasped her son Nazir to her bosom and tugged her playful daughters into the lift with her, one after another.

Leila chattered in voluble toddler-speak and Lucia listened, her little fingers twisting at her copper curls and her thumb creeping into her mouth until her mother pulled it out again. Nazir, replete after a feed, snored gently below his mother's chin.

'Auntie Maya,' Leila framed. 'Like Auntie Maya.'

'I should hope so.' Izzy was almost bouncing with excitement at the prospect of seeing her twin and the rest of her family.

It was their twenty-fourth birthday and Maya and Izzy were having a joint celebration at the Alihreza palace. Helicopters had been flying in all afternoon, ferrying loads of VIPs to the party being staged.

Having ascended the throne and become King, Rafiq had become less sensitive about his father's troubled legacy and the sleazy goings-on he had once associated with the desert building. After all, he and Izzy, their girls and their newborn son, Nazir, were now very much a family and Alihreza was the perfect place to unwind after a busy week of activity at the royal palace. It also provided an even more perfect backdrop for a large party because it offered plenty of luxurious accommodation for family members, who were staying on for a holiday.

Nazir had not been a planned baby. Traumatised by the twins' emergency birth, Rafiq had announced that two children were quite sufficient for them and that there was no way he would allow Izzy to risk herself again with a second pregnancy. Even though Izzy had wheeled in medical support to underline the truth that she had simply been unlucky and that twin pregnancies were more likely to encounter complications, Rafiq had taken an immoveable stance. That had been a shock to Izzy's system as usually Rafiq was willing to move heaven and earth just to give her whatever she wanted.

In fact, they had had heated discussions for weeks over whether or not they should have another child and then fate, that Rafiq was generally so fond of, had intervened and Izzy had discovered that she was expecting again. Of course, she wasn't taking contraceptive pills any longer because the several brands she had tried after the twins' birth hadn't agreed with her and Rafiq had taken charge of the contraception. She had been three months pregnant by the time she finally appreciated that once again she had conceived. She had been over-joyed by the surprise but Rafiq's reaction had been more shock and concern for her well-being.

Mercifully none of his fears had come to frui-tion during her second pregnancy. She had suffered minimal nausea and the delivery had been straight-forward. Happy now to consider their family com-plete, she was even more grateful for the fact that Nazir was a wonderfully easy, good-natured baby, who slept when he should, ate at regular hours and smiled beatifically at everyone.

Leila had needed very little sleep and after a few weeks of sleepless nights they had hired an official nanny. It had amazed Izzy that Lucia could slumber on peacefully even though she was only feet away from her screaming sibling. But the twins were very different, Izzy conceded fondly. Leila was altogether a louder personality, a little extrovert in the making. Copper-haired Lucia was quieter and prone to wandering off to amuse herself with imaginative games with her toys, leaving Leila the one to follow her. Leila went looking for her twin the minute she moved out of sight, but Lucia was more independent. Izzy loved seeing the children's different personalities emerging.

At that moment her mother, Lucia, walked up and stole Nazir out of her elder daughter's arms, rocking him and murmuring sweet nothings to the sleeping bundle. 'I swear an earthquake could go off and this child wouldn't notice!' she carolled appreciatively. 'Matt is so excited about being put forward for the stem cell treatment, Izzy. We'll never be able to thank Rafiq enough for doing that for him, even if it doesn't provide either an improvement of his condition or a miraculous cure.'

Izzy swallowed hard. It had been Rafiq who had suggested that they sought stem cell treatment for her kid brother's paralysis. Her family could never have afforded the costs involved. Matt had recently undergone a series of tests, which had concluded with him being offered a place in ground-breaking trials. She was married to a man with a huge heart, even if it was a heart that he often felt he had to bury deep and hide from notice, and if anything two years of marriage had only made her love her husband more deeply than ever. The happiness their relationship gave her was infinite.

Izzy watched as Rafiq snatched Leila back in the nick of time from the edge of an ornamental pond and scolded her. The little girl threw a massive tantrum and Rafiq just stood there watching it play out while Lucia sucked her thumb and stared. Izzy began to move in their direction. She gave her father a fond hug on the way, teased Matt about the latest piece of technology he was playing games with and greeted and kissed Rafiq's uncle and aunt on the cheek, pausing to chat with the older couple for a few minutes. By the end of it, Leila was still stubbornly going strong.

'Leila…' she intervened sharply.

The tantrum died with Izzy's arrival, but Leila ran off in a sulk instead, causing Rafiq to roll his eyes and groan out.

'It'll blow over,' Izzy told him soothingly. 'It's the result of too much excitement and the annoyance of me choosing what she had to wear today.'

'She's very wilful,' he said with a frown.

'She'll learn, just like we all have to learn how to behave,' Izzy countered. 'Just don't tell her any more stories about the warrior queen who preceded her in case it gives her ideas.'

Laughing, Rafiq tugged her back under an

archway onto the shaded terrace. 'You look pretty spectacular in that dress,' he remarked huskily. 'Dark blue suits you, matches your eyes.'

Izzy lounged back against a sandstone pillar and preened herself like an old-style sex siren, looking up at her husband cheekily from beneath her lashes. She leant closer to walk her fingertips up over his shirted abdomen, one at a time, the spirit of wantonness personified as she stroked his lean muscled torso, appreciating his physical beauty with every fibre of her being and loving that he was all hers for ever. She watched his gorgeous eyes light up as golden as the sun and noticed with a wicked little grin how he shifted position to contain his arousal.

'I married a shameless hussy.'

'And you love that shamelessness, Your Majesty,' she whispered, gazing up at him with her heart in her eyes.

'I do and I always will. I will cherish my memory of the virgin who told me not to be a party pooper for ever,' he husked, lowering his head to claim a single burning kiss that lit her up like a firework.

'I love you,' Izzy said sunnily, squeezing his hand. 'You may be a king but you're still my bathroom guy...'

Rafiq winced. 'Are you ever going to let me forget our first meeting?'

'Probably not.' She laughed as they joined the festivities to mingle and chat and ensure that their guests had as good a time as they planned to have for the rest of their lives.

* * * * *

Lost in the magic of Cinderella's Royal Secret *by Lynne Graham?*

Look out for the final instalment in the Cinderella Brides for Billionaires duet, Maya and Raffaele's story, coming soon!

And why not explore these other Lynne Graham stories?

His Cinderella's One-Night Heir
The Greek's Surprise Christmas Bride
Indian Prince's Hidden Son
The Innocent's Forgotten Wedding

Available now

#3829 CLAIMING HIS UNKNOWN SON
Spanish Secret Heirs
by Kim Lawrence
Marisa was the first and last woman Roman Bardales proposed to, and her stark refusal turned his heart to stone. Now he's finally discovered the lasting effects of their encounter: his son! And he's about to stake his claim to his child...

#3830 A FORBIDDEN NIGHT WITH THE HOUSEKEEPER
by Heidi Rice
Maxim Durand can't believe that housekeeper Cara has inherited *his* vineyard. But bartering with the English beauty isn't going to be simple... As their desire explodes into passionate life, the question is: What does Maxim want? His rightful inheritance... or Cara?

#3831 HER WEDDING NIGHT NEGOTIATION
by Chantelle Shaw
Kindhearted Leah Ashbourne's wedding *has* to go ahead to save her mother from ruin. So the collapse of her engagement is a disaster! Until billionaire Marco arrives, needing her help. Leah is ready to negotiate with him—but her price is marriage!

#3832 REVELATIONS OF HIS RUNAWAY BRIDE
by Kali Anthony
From the moment Thea Lambros is forced to walk down the aisle toward Christo Callas, her only thought is escape. But when coolly brilliant Christo interrupts her getaway, Thea meets her electrifying match. Because her new husband unleashes an unexpected fire within her...

———————

YOU CAN FIND MORE INFORMATION ON UPCOMING HARLEQUIN TITLES, FREE EXCERPTS AND MORE AT HARLEQUIN.COM.

HPCNMRB0620

*From the moment Thea Lambros is forced to walk
down the aisle toward Christo Callas, her only thought
is escape. But when coolly brilliant Christo interrupts
her getaway, Thea meets her electrifying match.
Because her new husband unleashes an unexpected
fire within her…*

*Read on for a sneak preview of
Kali Anthony's debut story for Harlequin Presents,*
Revelations of His Runaway Bride.

"This marriage is a sham."

In some ways, he agreed with her. Yet here he stood, with a gold
wedding band prickling on his finger. Thea still held her rings. He
needed her to put them on. If she did, he'd have won—for tonight.

"You're asking me to return you to the tender care of your
father?" A man Christo suspected didn't have a sentimental, loving
bone in his body.

Thea grabbed the back of a spindly chair, clutching it till her
fingers blanched. "I'm asking you to let me go."

"No."

Christo had heard whispers about Tito Lambros. He was
reported to be cruel and vindictive. The bitter burn of loathing
coursed like poison through his veins. That his father's negligence
had allowed such a man to hold Christo's future in his hands…

There was a great deal he needed to learn about Thea's family—
some of which he might be able to use. But that could wait. Now it
was time to give her something to cling to. Hope.

"You'll come with me as my wife and we'll discuss the situation
in which we find ourselves. That's my promise. But we're leaving
now."

She looked down at her clothes and back at him. Her liquid amber eyes glowed in the soft lights. "I can't go dressed like this!"

No more delays. She glanced at the door again. He didn't want a scene. Her tantrums could occur at his home, where any witnesses would be paid to hold their silence.

"You look perfect," he said, waving his hand in her direction. "It shows a flair for the dramatic—which you've proved to have in abundance tonight. Our exit will be unforgettable."

She seemed to compose herself. Thrust her chin high, all glorious defiance. "But my hat… I told everyone about it. I can't disappoint them."

"Life's full of disappointments. Tell them it wouldn't fit over your magnificent hair."

Thea's lips twitched in a barely suppressed sneer, her eyes narrow and glacial. The look she threw him would have slayed a mere mortal. Luckily, for the most part, he felt barely human.

"Rings," he said.

She jammed them carelessly onto her finger. Victory. He held out the crook of his arm and she hesitated before slipping hers through it. All stiff and severe. But her body still fitted into his in a way that enticed him. Caused his heart to thrum, his blood to roar. Strange. Intoxicating. All Thea.

"Now smile," he said.

She plastered on a mocking grimace.

He leaned down and whispered in her ear, "Like you mean it, *koukla mou*."

"I'll smile when you say that like you mean it, Christo."

And he laughed.

This second laugh was more practiced. More familiar—like an old memory. But the warmth growing in his chest was real. Beyond all expectations, he was enjoying her. For his sanity, perhaps a little too much…

Don't miss
Revelations of His Runaway Bride
available July 2020 wherever
Harlequin Presents books and ebooks are sold.

Harlequin.com

HPEXP0620